FAUST

SHADOWRIDGE GUARDIANS MC, BOOK 8

PEPPER NORTH

PHOTOGRAPHY BY
JW PHOTOGRAPHY

COVER MODEL
ALFIE GORDILLO

CHAPTER
ONE

Something that sounded like a slow hiss caught her attention. Molly turned off her radio and strained to listen. Shoot! That glass she'd driven over appeared to have cut her tire. Wondering if she would be lucky enough to get home before it was too flat, Molly slowed down as she debated how far she could go.

When she heard a thump from the front tire, she knew she needed to stop. Easing over on the side of the highway and stopping under one of the big lights illuminating the pavement, she debated what to do. She could have called one of the elders from the church during the day. They would have helped her but at two in the morning, that wasn't possible. They'd have too many questions for her she didn't want to answer. Suddenly, going to that late movie in the town down the road seemed like a bad decision.

"Okay! You've got a spare tire and a jack," Molly told herself. "You can do this."

She turned to look around her car, checking for traffic. One solitary truck drove past on the other side of the divided highway. Did she want someone to help her? That seemed dangerous on the deserted road in the dark.

After blowing out a deep breath, Molly launched into action. She opened her door and pushed the trunk release on the small hatchback. Racing to the back to get out of the road, she pushed the hatch fully up and leaned inside to push the church bulletins for next Sunday to the side. She pulled up the spare tire cover and stared down at it.

By the time she had it unfastened from its mooring spot, Molly was already doubting her ability to change this tire. "Never give up!" She attempted to rally her positivity.

"Uf!" The heavy tire moved about three inches as she heaved it toward the opening. Maybe she should work on getting the other tire off. That might be the first step. The jack was lighter to pull out of the car anyway.

Referring to the manual, she searched with her fingers looking for the spot it recommended to place the jack. Not able to find it, Molly stretched out on the shoulder, feeling the gritty gravel and who knows what else that had gathered there.

"Aha! There it is! I just needed to see from a better angle." Her voice sounded really loud in the quiet that surrounded her. "I really need to stop talking to myself." That sounded even louder, sending a shiver down her spine.

A few minutes of success later, she looked at the tire now suspended off the pavement with satisfaction. She grabbed the tire iron and fitted it onto a lug nut. Giving it a spin, she yelped when it whacked her shin as the tire rotated freely around.

"Okay, that's just mean. How are you supposed to get the tire unfastened if it's spinning?"

Back to the manual she went and discovered she'd skipped one important step. Molly had just started trying to lower the jack when she heard the rumble of oncoming motorcycles. She looked across the road hoping they were on the other side. "Of course, not."

Her hands tightened on the tire iron as the bikes pulled over in front and behind her car. "They're friendly. I'm sure they just look mean."

"Need some help?" a rough voice called as he kicked his stand down and swung his leg over the seat.

"No. No, thank you. I'm figuring it out," she rushed to assure them as everyone followed his example.

"It doesn't look like you've got it quite mastered yet," that gruff voice said sarcastically.

Molly backed up slightly to the edge of the shoulder to keep the men advancing from both sides in her view. Her heels teetered on the edge, so she took a baby step forward to maintain her balance. A glance behind her showed a sloping drop off into tangled weeds. She shuddered at the thought of the creepy crawlers hanging out there.

"She's definitely polite."

"I like being pleasant. I will warn you that my cheerfulness is almost gone. Perhaps you should just leave." Tears prickled her eyelids. She was tired, dirty, and scared. Molly had no idea how to change a tire and she really didn't want to know how. Now, some bikers were here to kill her. Could this day get any worse? She wiped a hand over each eye to wipe away the tears before they could fall and tried to keep her shoulders from sagging in defeat.

"What's your name?" that gruff voice asked.

A scuff on the gravel made Molly turn to look at him, and she jumped in surprise to see how close he was to her already. He was tall and muscular with tattoos that proclaimed him to be a very bad man. What made her stare was the dead look in his eyes. This man didn't care about anything.

Tears coursed down her cheeks as she tried to convince herself they wouldn't harm her. "Please, leave me alone. Don't hurt me."

A noise on the other side made her jerk her head that way to see who was approaching. This guy was younger. He didn't look as cruel, but even Molly could spot knives tucked into strategic places. She took a step back and felt her heel slide again on the gravel. Lurching forward, she rebalanced herself before looking back and forth between the two men.

"Whoa, Little girl. We're not going to hurt you. We'll help with your tire and send you on your way," the stone-faced man promised. The dead tone of his voice got Molly. What had this man suffered to reach this place where he felt nothing?

Without meaning to, Molly rushed forward to wrap her arms around his waist and hug him tight.

She knew something was seriously wrong when all the noise died out completely. Looking up, she released him and took a big step back only to teeter once again on the edge of the shoulder. Realizing it was a lost cause to fight it, Molly relaxed her muscles hoping not to break something as she fell.

"Eep!" burst from her lips as the man reached out to lift her back to safety as effortlessly as steadying a toy.

"Eep?" he repeated.

"Sorry. Thank you." Molly rubbed her eyes once again to make sure no tears had escaped.

"Come stand over here by the back of your car. The guys can change your tire. They love doing good deeds," the man who'd prevented her tumble shared with a sarcastic tone.

"That's so nice of them. I should go thank them," Molly stammered, not quite sure how she should handle the elephant in the room, so to speak. The hug.

"No way. You're standing right here next to me."

"C—Could you tell me your name?" she asked, knowing she'd ignored a request for hers. "I'm Molly."

"Faust."

"Like the man who made a pact with the devil?" Molly asked.

"Yes."

She could hear the men swearing at the mechanics who'd tightened the lug nuts so tight while the others lounged carelessly on their bikes. The silence between her and Faust seemed almost deafening. She had to say something.

"The minister says I need to stop hugging people."

"He's a smart man obviously."

Again, that dratted lull. She peeked up at Faust and found him studying her. "I don't hug that many people. Only those who I know need a hug."

"And I needed a hug?" he drawled.

She couldn't tell from his expression if he was angry or amused.

"Are you mad at me? I'm sorry if I made you uncomfortable."

"I'm not mad."

A few seconds later, she had to know. "Just surprised?"

"Definitely."

"The minister says I don't look like a hugger. Not that I hug that many people."

"Just those who need one."

"Right!" She smiled at him. He understood.

He stared at her harder than ever. He didn't understand. She took an automatic step forward then forced herself to stop. He might forgive her for hugging him once. Twice would be way over the top.

She felt for her necklace. It wasn't anything special. A plain cross on a fake gold chain. Molly had gotten it from her grandmother when she was twelve and skipped school to be a cool kid. It was a reminder that her path wasn't to be cool. Her path was to do the right thing.

Like hugs.

She knew cool people didn't go around hugging tough looking bikers whether they needed one or not. Most people probably were scared of them—like she had been when they'd first rolled up. Molly looked over at the two guys working together to change her tire. They had the old one off and were pulling the spare out of her trunk.

"She's just got a donut, Faust," the one with a tangled mane of beautiful hair called.

Molly tried not to covet his hair. Hers was mousy brown and ordinary. Kind of like her brown eyes and thin face. She peeked up at Faust. His face was all hard angles. She'd tried not to notice his body, but the hug had cemented in her mind that his strength was bone deep. Suddenly, she wondered if he liked banana pudding.

He turned and walked away just as she'd almost gotten brave enough to ask. She watched him head back to his bike and felt sad. He was tired of talking to her. Of course, he was.

Plain Molly. Oh, she could doll herself up. Or at least she had on a few occasions before she started working at the church. She'd looked okay with some camouflage from makeup. But she'd always felt like she was deceiving people. Shouldn't they like her without a bunch of stuff all over her skin?

Shaking her head at her thoughts, Molly looked back at Faust. He'd seemed like a nice biker. A mean guy would have let her fall. And he hadn't even made a big deal when she'd hugged him.

Peeking back over, she saw him lean over and search through one of the leather bags attached to each side of his bike. Molly immediately looked down at her feet after noticing his—assets. Scuffing her shoes in the gravel, she waited for the men to finish her car so she could thank them, without hugs, and go hide in her apartment.

A dark brown teddy bear appeared in front of her. Automatically, she reached out to touch it. "It's so cute. I love his expression."

"This is for you," Faust said, handing her the stuffie.

"Oh. I can't take this. I've already made a fool of myself."

"Every Little girl needs a friend."

"Little girl?" she repeated as she took the bear. Molly studied the biker's face as she hugged the bear to her chest.

"Think of it as an exchange. A bear for a hug."

"Thank you." She knew she looked sappy with tears in her eyes, but she couldn't believe he wanted to give her something.

This time she didn't even try to wipe them away. It was okay if he knew.

"The guys are almost finished. Your spare is a donut. It won't go fast, and it won't go far. Get your tire replaced soon. Do you know how to buy tires?"

"I can ask the minister. There's probably someone in the congregation who can help me."

"If not, come to the Shadowridge Guardian's shop. We'll help you," Faust told her.

"Oh, that's very kind of you." Molly stopped herself from hugging him. *Really?*

"We're all done, miss," the man with the beautiful hair told her as he cleaned his hands on a rag.

"Tell me your name, please," Molly asked, daring to smile at him.

"Blade."

She nodded like the dangerous name was perfectly normal. "And you?"

"Storm."

"Thank you, gentlemen."

The men both looked at her sharply at her use of that term. Faust spoke up. "You can be gentlemen for five minutes without spontaneously combusting."

Storm studied Faust's defensive posture in front of Molly and nodded. "You're welcome, miss."

"Drive home safely," another biker called as they all headed back to their rides.

"Thank you all!" she called loudly and winced as her voice resounded in the quiet evening air.

"Go get in your car, Molly," Faust urged. "I'll make sure you get to town."

"Oh! Yes. I need to get home. Thanks again. And sorry!"

CHAPTER
TWO

Faust watched the young woman walk back to her car. She got in and leaned to the right to do something in the passenger seat. Was she buckling the teddy bear in? Definitely. That's what she was up to. With that task done, he heard her start the engine before waiting. As if he could read her mind, he knew what she was thinking.

"Clubhouse," he called to his brothers.

She was so nervous about being around them. The last thing they needed was to have her ram into someone when she hit the gas instead of the brakes. He watched Molly turn to see all the motorcycles pass her but one.

Molly waited to see if he would take off, but Faust simply flashed his headlights at her. She lurched to a start and Faust knew he had rattled her. He was used to making people nervous. He'd rather people avoided him. It was easier. Faust didn't allow himself to wonder why he felt bad about scaring her.

That hug ricocheted into his mind as he followed her down the road. Who'd hug a biker on the side of the road after dark? Someone who saw the best in people. She'd said he looked like he needed a hug.

Molly.

The car ahead drove slowly on the spare. When they reached the outskirts of town, he flashed his lights at her again and peeled off for the clubhouse. He tried to keep himself from tracking her in his side mirror. That didn't work.

When she'd disappeared from view, he revved the engine and sped off. He'd never see her again. That bothered him.

Pulling into the Shadowridge Guardians' compound, he drove to the parking lot and backed into a space. He could hear the music going and knew Talon had to be teaching the Littles how to dance again.

There'd always been old ladies at the club house. There still were a couple, but the motorcycle club's refuge had taken a new tone lately. Faust would never admit it, but he envied them. Not that he'd ever find a Little who'd want to hook up with him. He was sure that Blade with his bad boy good looks would be much more appealing.

Pissed at that thought, he swung his leg over his bike and jerked free the strap of his helmet. Slamming it down on his seat, he stalked into the clubhouse.

"Want to come dance with us, Faust?" Ivy asked.

"No."

"Oh, okay," Ivy said, looking hurt by his snapping tone.

Faust could see Steele tense and push away from the wall. Shaking his head, Faust apologized, "Sorry, Ivy. It's been a long day."

"Oh. I'm sorry, too." She smiled at him and added, "Tomorrow is going to be better. Did you help that woman get home?"

"I made sure she got back to town."

"That was nice of you all to stop and help her," Harper chimed in.

"You gave her a bear?" Elizabeth asked, abandoning the dance floor to join the growing circle of Little girls around Faust.

"I think your Daddy wants to dance," Faust pointed out.

"Oh, he really doesn't. He volunteered to entertain us until you got back to tell us all the deets," Remi asked, before pulling her bubble gum partially out of her mouth to twirl around her finger.

Faust rubbed his hand over his head and looked at their Daddies who observed with grins. "No deets. Molly had a flat. We stopped to help her. I gave her a bear because I thought she might like one. Storm and Blade changed her tire. I followed her back to town."

"You thought she might like a bear?" Carlee asked with a grin.

"We didn't know you were psychic, Faust," Atlas commented.

"Fuck off, Atlas," Faust snarled.

"Ooo! That's more money for the swear jar." Eden ran off toward library.

"Walk, Little girl," Gabriel ordered.

Eden peeked over her shoulder after slowing down. "Sorry, Daddy." She skipped the rest of the way there and back.

"Ten dollars, please," Eden chirped, holding the jar bulging with bills up for Faust to add his contribution to.

"I thought it was five," he growled as he reached for his money clip in his front pocket.

"Inflation," Addie suggested.

"And you used the F word. That's double," Remi pointed out.

"Right." Faust put his hands on his hips and tried to stare her down. Remi didn't blink.

"Her name was Molly? And she hugged you?" Elizabeth asked.

"Seems like some Daddies around here have loose lips. I thought what happened between brothers stayed between brothers," Faust said, glaring at the men who'd all now gathered close.

"Ten dollars, please," Eden reminded him, holding the jar a bit higher.

Faust shook his head and carefully peeled off the required amount from his money roll. He pressed it gently into the jar. He didn't want to hurt any of the Littles, especially Eden. She hadn't been with Bear too long.

"So, she hugged you?" Harper asked.

"Yes. She hugged me. It didn't mean anything. She said the minister told her to stop hugging people," Faust exploded, causing the Littles to back up closer to their Daddies.

"Faust..." Bear warned.

"The minister. So, she's religious," Elizabeth noted.

Ivy pulled a small notebook out of her pocket and wrote something carefully.

"What are you doing, Little girl?" Steele asked before Faust could.

"Oh, we want to find Molly for Faust," Carlee explained. "We're taking notes. Did she have any striking characteristics? A lisp? A limp? A missing limb?"

"What? No," Faust said, looking at Carlee. He didn't know what to do with her. A missing limb? That's fucked up. "She was perfectly well formed."

"Oooo!" the Little girls said in unison. Ivy added that to her notes.

"Welcome to the world of Littles, Faust," Steele said, holding up his hand for a fist bump.

Faust just shook his head.

"You can't leave Daddy hanging!" Ivy protested and practically climbed Steele to bang her fist against her Daddy's before turning to glare at Faust.

Faust found himself apologizing before he even knew what he was doing. He didn't apologize. For anything.

"That's okay, Faust. You had a close encounter of the hug kind today. That's got to set you a bit wacky." Ivy forgave him and took advantage of being in Steele's arms to rest her head on his shoulder. "We'll forgive you if you give me more information to add to our notes."

"Little girl. You are not to search for Molly. Leave that to Faust. He can find her," Steele told her before looking at him. "That Morningside Methodist Church sticker in the window might help you, Faust."

"Oooo!" the Littles said together again. Ivy dug her pad and pen out of her pocket and tossed it to Eden to add that to the notes.

"Thanks, Steele. I hadn't noticed that at all." Faust turned and stalked through the clubhouse to his apartment.

He forced himself not to pull his phone out of his pocket until he reached the privacy of his rooms. Closing the door, he leaned against it and did a quick search. It was in a good area. Hopefully, she lived close by. He'd go visit the church tomorrow.

He wouldn't spontaneously combust if he stepped into a church. Would he? More likely, they'd chase him out with pitch forks.

Let them try.

Faust jumped in the shower and washed the day off. He worked getting the ground in motorcycle grease off his hands. It seemed to weld itself in his skin as he worked each day to make motors growl. He realized he was stressing too much when his skin looked more red than sparkly clean. Pulling on a fresh pair of jeans and a T-shirt, he stopped for a minute to spread some thick cream on his abused hands.

Molly would either accept that he was a working man, or she wouldn't. He couldn't change who he was at the core. He hadn't seen a glint of disdain in her beautiful brown eyes, but Faust had run into plenty of women who liked a ride on the wild side and didn't have any intention of having a permanent relationship with a motorcycle mechanic.

He walked out his door and closed it with a restrained click before stalking to the kitchen to find something to eat. He'd already missed lunch and was a couple hours late for dinner. That was one good thing about the clubhouse. There was always food.

Bear greeted him with, "There's chili on the stove."

"Cheese dip over here," Carlee told him.

"Yum. I think I could put those two together."

Faust never worried about calories. His long lean body ate them up as he worked hard all day. Grabbing a plate, he scattered corn chips over it, added some chili, and raided the cheese dip to drizzle a bit over his concoction. Sitting down at a table, he met Atlas's gaze and nodded when the bartender offered him a beer.

"I'll go." Ivy jumped to her feet and ran over to collect the can.

Faust was thankful to see her walk sedately back to his side. There wouldn't be a shaken-up beer explosion tonight. "Thank you, Ivy."

"I didn't shake it up this time on accident. Thanks for trusting me to bring you one."

"Of course, Ivy. There's not a mean bone in your body," Faust said, popping the top on the beer. He took a drink before scooping up a bite of his nacho creation.

Blade wandered from the bar with a fresh beer as well and settled down next to him. "Hey, I wanted to talk to you about that old bike I bought to work on."

"What about it?" Faust studied Blade.

"I know you're a magician with engines, but it sounded so bad today coming in I didn't know whether I'd make it to the shop. Is it worth rebuilding that engine or am I better off getting a new one?"

"Let me look at it tomorrow. Sometimes the sound is just an adjustment thing. Or it could be metal shaving in the oil. Then you're screwed," Faust told him.

"I did check the oil when I bought it. It was definitely past its prime," Blade told him. "Thanks, Faust. I know you're busy."

Faust met his gaze directly. "I'll make time for another Guardian."

Blade nodded his thanks. "If I can help you with any weaponry, let me know."

Nodding, Faust took another bite. "Thank you for helping my Little girl with her tire."

"Yours, huh?"

"Not a doubt about it," Faust confirmed and studied Blade's face to see if he had a problem with that.

"I love how fate put someone special in front of you. Maybe it will happen for me," Blade commented lightly.

The two men sat quietly for a few minutes listening to the Littles chatting and having fun. They were currently involved in a game of "I Spy" and having a great time. It was entertaining to see what they picked to have the others guess. Several cuddled their teddy bears. Steele babysat Ivy's at the bar. Faust noticed he held it very carefully as if he'd been taught how to take care of the precious stuffie.

"You going to find her tomorrow?" Blade asked.

"I'd go tonight but I don't want to scare her," Faust answered.

"She hugged you, big guy. I don't think she's scared of you."

CHAPTER
THREE

Letting herself into the quiet church, Molly walked as silently as possible across the carpeted floor to the office. She loved her job working as the church secretary. It was definitely more interesting than she'd expected. Even trying to avoid gossip and sensitive information, she had a front row seat to all the drama and intrigue that any large group of people brought with them.

After unlocking the door, she set down her purse and tote bag on her desk and walked to the refrigerator to put away her lunch. Molly was always the first person to arrive. She liked being there to get prepared before her day started. The last stop was to fill the coffee pot tank for everyone to brew their favorites before heading back to her desk.

Opening her laptop, she pressed the start button and turned to the phone. The red message light already flashed on her phone. Crossing her fingers that it was not bad news, Molly grabbed a pad of paper and a pen before reviewing the calls that had come in.

One made her stop and call the minister. "Steve? It's Molly."

"Hi, Molly. Already hard at work? I should be there in fifteen minutes or so," the kindly older man told her.

"You may wish to go straight over to the nursing home. I have a message that came in ten minutes ago. Adele Kelly is not expected to make it through the next few hours," Molly told him, trying to keep the tears that streamed down her face from affecting her speech.

"Bless, Adele. One of my favorites—but don't tell anyone I have a few in the flock I like more than others," the minister requested.

"Never, sir. She is one of my non-favorites, too."

"Everyone's probably. Thanks for calling. You're right. I want to get there to ease her passage and comfort the family. Hold down the fort for me, Molly."

"Will do, sir," she promised before rushing ahead to ask, "I hate to even ask but I had a flat last night. Do we have anyone who deals with tires?"

"Let me think. I'll send you a message if anyone comes to my mind."

"Thanks, sir. Please tell Adele's family that she is so loved," Molly requested.

"I'll tell them."

When he disconnected, Molly wiped the tears from her cheeks. She tried to think of all the happy memories she had of the sweet woman who'd come to sit in the front row for years. Every time Molly talked to her, Adele had mentioned her late husband. She'd missed him for so many years.

A fresh wave of tears welled to her eyes, and she grabbed for a handful of Kleenex. She hated to lose Adele but knew the sweet woman would soon be reunited with her husband.

The door jangled and she tried to pull herself together. Dabbing at her eyes, she babbled, "So sorry. Bad news on the messages this morning." Looking up, she saw the fiercely hand-some biker who'd taken care of her last night. Without thinking, she stood and held up her arms to him, silently asking for a hug.

He didn't say a word, just walked past the long counter and through the swinging gate. He dropped his helmet on her desk before striding around it to scoop her up in his arms. Faust sat down with her cuddled on his lap. Molly loved that he didn't ask any questions but just held her against his powerful body. She heard the rustle of her plastic tote bag then felt the soft fur of the stuffie she hadn't been able to leave at home.

"Thank you," she sobbed and hid her face in the curve of his neck. Molly closed her eyes at the feel of his hand stroking through her hair. He didn't say trite phrases like "there, there" or "it will be okay." Faust just held her and let her cry.

After several minutes, she pulled herself together. "I'm so sorry. You must think I'm a mess."

He reached with one long arm for a tissue and wiped her face. "I think you live with your heart wide open. Very few people are brave enough to do that. And, for the record, you're fucking hot whether your nose is a bit red or not."

"Molly! What are you doing in here?" The assistant minister looked at her like she was the devil incarnate.

"You will not talk to her like that." The statement grated from Faust's lips sounding harsh and deadly.

Faust didn't move. He continued to hold her in his arms, rocking her office chair from side to side.

"Is that a threat? I'm calling the police," Lester O'Brien stated as he juggled all the stuff in his arms to reach his phone in his pocket.

"Adele is dying," Molly told him before sitting up to whisper to Faust, "Thank you for comforting me."

After helping Molly to her feet, Faust stood as well. He hesitated before awkwardly handing Molly the wad of tissues in his hand for her to finish the job. Molly smiled at him as she accepted his gift. She loved that Faust made no move to leave and absolutely paid no attention to the challenging assistant minister.

"Molly. Who is that man?" Lester demanded before hissing, "And how could you think it would be acceptable to be canoodling in the church's office?"

"Back off," Faust barked.

To Molly's delight, the skinny man took several steps away from her desk. She told herself she shouldn't enjoy seeing him so uncomfortable.

"Mr. O'Brien, this is Faust. He's a Shadowridge Guardian. I had a flat tire last night and Faust and his…"

"Brothers," Faust supplied for her.

"Faust and his brothers stopped in the middle of the dark highway and changed my tire for me. He came by to check on me this morning and found me upset. Minister Steve is on his way to the nursing home now," Molly explained.

"Minister Zigler." Lester corrected her usage of his first name.

"Our head religious leader has asked everyone in the congregation to call him Minister Steve. I will follow his instructions," Molly said, setting her stuffie on her desk next to Faust's helmet.

"Never mind. He needs to leave. I will suggest that Minister Zigler counsel you in the appropriate way a young woman should behave. Because this is not it."

Faust took a few steps forward to stand toe to toe with the judgmental man. "You will not talk to Molly in that tone. I will not ask you again."

"Or what? You're going to punch me?" Lester asked, challenging him.

"Do you need bruises to be nice to someone? That seems to go against biblical law," Faust answered, leaning slightly forward to lurk over him.

"Like you know anything about the bible."

"'Do unto others as you would have them do unto you.' Matthew 7:12."

Faust heard a giggle from behind him as the sanctimonious man's mouth dropped open. "Don't challenge people you know nothing about. It doesn't end well. And never doubt that I am a man of my word. I will hurt you if you don't treat Molly as the amazing person she is."

The man sputtered, obviously struggling to respond to that assurance.

"Lester, I put some paperwork on your desk last night before I went home. Could you look that over and see what the church would like to do with the information?" Molly asked, giving him an out.

Almost walking backward to keep Faust in view, the man scurried down the short hallway and darted into his office. Lester closed his door with a bang. There was no mistaking the click of the lock engaging.

"Is he always like that?" Faust asked sharply.

Shrugging, Molly tried to brush off the question. "Was there a reason you came to see me today?"

"I wanted to check on your tire."

"You tracked me here—because of my tire?" she asked. "How did you find me anyway?"

"There's a sticker in your back window. Give me your keys and I'll take your car to get the tire changed." Faust held out his hand.

This time it was Molly's mouth that dropped open. "I can't ask you to do that. Besides…"

When her voice trailed off, Faust understood. A church secretary couldn't make a lot of money. "Give me your phone."

Without even asking why, Molly grabbed her purse and rummaged in it to find her phone. "Oh, it's almost dead. In all the excitement, I forgot to plug it in."

She handed it to Faust who noted the red indicator at the top. Faust opened her contacts and added his information before calling himself. Returning the device, he asked, "Do you have a charger?"

Molly set her phone back on her desk and started pulling things out of her purse. Faust watched in amazement as a pile grew. He noticed she tucked a tampon under a few other things so he wouldn't see it. Her cheeks turned a rosy pink.

Finally, she admitted defeat. "I don't. It's okay. I have a land-line here."

"Keys."

"Really, I'll get it taken care of by the end of the week."

Faust said nothing but stood there with his hand out. Finally, she relented and moved a few things in the jumble on her desk to find her keys. Placing them on his palm, she looked worried.

"Your car is safe with me, Molly."

"I'm not worried about that." She searched his face before adding, "Why are you doing this?"

"Because you're mine, Little girl. What did you name the bear?"

"Yours?" she repeated.

"Mine."

"You can't know that," Molly whispered.

He just raised one eyebrow as he looked at her. Did she really think he didn't recognize his Little? "What's your stuffie's name, Pixie?"

"Angel."

Faust snorted and nodded. "That's perfect. I'm going to leave my motorcycle here. Will you keep the asshole from having it towed?"

She started to laugh and controlled the urge. Her voice held a warble of amusement as she assured him, "I'll make sure it's safe."

"Thank you. I'll have your car back soon."

Molly rushed around her desk to hug him. Faust pulled her tightly against him, holding her close for several long seconds before stepping back. Immediately, he missed the feel of her. Shaking his head in disbelief, headed for the door and forced himself to not look back.

CHAPTER
FOUR

Molly tried to tune out the assistant minister's snide comments all morning as she worked. By the time their boss arrived, she was ready to pull her hair out. Immediately, her thoughts returned to the kind lady he'd gone to visit.

"Is she…" Molly asked.

"Adele is gone. Her family and I were at her side. It was peaceful," the minister assured her.

Blinking away the tears, Molly nodded. "I went through all the other messages and set a few notes on your desk." She heard the slam of a door opening so vigorously it banged against the wall. "Oh…"

"Steve, you need to get rid of this woman," Lester blathered over her.

"Get rid of Molly? The church would fall apart without her," her boss answered. "Besides, the parishioners would not be happy."

"They would if they'd been here this morning to see her conduct with that tattooed biker. I walked in to see her sitting on his lap!" The man's tone increased with each word to a final shout of indignation.

"That does not sound like our Molly," the minister observed, turning to look at Molly.

"He walked in just after I'd gotten off the phone with you. I was upset," she tried to explain. "Like I told you earlier, I had a flat tire last night. The Shadowridge Guardians MC came to my rescue. One of the bikers talked to me while two of his brothers put my donut on."

"How nice of them to stop and help you."

"It was. I was scared at first, but they took care of my tire in minutes. I liked them."

"And one of them came to your rescue again?" the minister asked with a smile.

"Yes, Faust came in this morning to offer to fix my tire. I was upset after getting off the phone with you. He didn't ask any questions but comforted me."

"Comforted," Lester snorted and received a disapproving look from the head minister.

"This is the same man who helped you last night?" Steve asked, refocusing their conversation.

"It was. He saw the church sticker in my window." Molly smiled. The stickers had been her idea to advertise the church.

"And now there's a motorcycle in the parking lot. That could scare off new churchgoers," Lester observed.

"That's Faust's. He took my car to get a tire to replace the donut. I told him I'd take care of it, but he insisted," Molly told him.

"Faust, hmmm. I think I'll like this guy. The Shadowridge Guardians MC are known for doing some good things for the community. They're also known for not hesitating to bend the rules. Be careful, Molly."

"I will," Molly promised.

"I'll go work on those messages," Steve said, finishing the conversation. "Lester, did you get all the volunteers you needed for the chili competition after church next weekend?"

"I'm still working on it," Lester admitted.

"That should be your first priority for today. Molly, need anything from me?"

"There are some bills for your approval, but they can wait until you have a free minute," she answered quickly.

"Thank you, Molly. Let's get busy." Steve waited until Lester turned to walk into his office before entering his.

Molly collapsed into her chair. Lester always was unpleasant, but he'd never threatened her job. She picked up Angel and hugged her close. "It's going to be okay," she whispered before forcing herself to tuck the stuffie back into her tote bag.

As she shifted the motorcycle helmet to the side of her desk, she caught a whiff of Faust's distinctive scent. Leaning forward she inhaled again and felt her body's reaction. Molly squeezed her legs together as she felt herself becoming wet. She rubbed the top before forcing herself to get to work.

Grabbing her own checklist for the chili cookoff from her in process clipboard, Molly noticed that Lester had written on her sheet.

Find twenty volunteers.

She rolled her eyes. This wasn't the first time he'd dumped a job on her. Molly always did whatever he didn't. It was easier that way and she made sure the church event went off smoothly. He'd obviously added that to her list the evening before and didn't think of mentioning to the head minister that he'd asked her to cover for him.

Pulling up her church directory, she scanned the names and started making calls. She had twenty people quickly. Jotting their names down in a post, she sent them to Lester without any comment.

Just before lunch, the door opened and Faust strode in. He commanded a room, seeming to occupy all the space. She stood up and forced herself to not to dart to hug him.

"Faust, hi!"

"Your car's back in its space with fresh tires in place."

"Tires?" she echoed.

"They were one sharp rock away from springing a leak." He held out her keys.

Molly looked down and thought furiously. She was never going to afford to pay him back. "Faust, I'm sorry. I don't have money for four new tires. Is there a way I can do something at your shop to work to pay back the money? If you'll let me pay you back over time." Molly crossed her fingers, hoping he wouldn't be mad.

"No charge, Little girl. The shop owed me a favor. You're all set," Faust assured her. He leaned forward and set her keys on her desk before bracing one hand on the desk to look into her eyes. "Taking care of you is your Daddy's job."

She nodded before she even processed what she was agreeing to. As his words registered fully on her mind, Molly felt her cheeks heat. Darting a glance around the room, she double-checked that her bosses were still in their offices. "You just met me, Faust. You can't be this sure we're supposed to be together."

He simply looked at her for a few seconds. "I'm off to work. I'll be at the shop for a few extra hours tonight. Will you go out with me tomorrow?"

"Yes."

"I'll pick you up at five. Write your address down for me," he directed.

Molly grabbed a pad of sticky notes and wrote down her address. After handing it to him, she watched Faust thrust the note into his jean pocket. Unable to stop, she considered the considerable bulge that filled his worn soft jeans.

His fingers under her chin tilted her head up until their gazes meshed. "Five o'clock tomorrow. If something happens before then, call me."

Nodding her agreement, Molly dropped her focus to his full sensuous lips. She bet he knew how to kiss. Withing thinking, she licked her lips and heard him groan softly. Her gaze rebounded to meet his.

"You're killing me, Little girl. Be good."

She nodded, willing to promise him anything. Being good was easy.

"You must be the thoughtful man who helped our Molly with her tire last night."

Molly looked quickly to see Steve standing in the doorway of his office. He walked forward and held out his hand to shake Faust's.

"Minister Steve, this is Faust. Faust, this is the amazing leader of this church, Steve Zigler." Molly quickly made introductions as the men shook hands.

"Steve," Faust greeted him brusquely. "I need to get to work."

Faust grabbed his helmet from her desk and turned to leave. He froze and pulled a cord from his back pocket. Turning back to her, he held out the charger. "Plug your phone in."

"Yes, Faust. Thank you." Molly was very touched. He'd made a special stop so she could charge her phone. She walked forward to hug him and grinned when he returned her squeezing embrace. When she stepped back, he was gone in seconds.

"That's an interesting man, Molly," Steve suggested.

Molly knew he was warning her. "He's unlike anyone I've ever met before."

"He threatened to punch me," Lester chimed in, acting brave now that Faust was gone.

"Only if you don't speak nicely to me. Avoiding being hit is totally possible," Molly clarified.

"We should all speak to each other politely. It shouldn't take a promise of physicality to get us to do so." Minister Steve looked at Lester meaningfully.

"Of course not. Matthew 7:12 and all that," Lester said righteously.

Molly couldn't prevent rolling her eyes as he quoted the same biblical verse that Faust had used. She quickly changed the subject.

"Do you have time to talk to me now, Steve?"

"This is the perfect time," the supportive minister agreed.

CHAPTER
FIVE

Swamped, Faust didn't even look up when the others finished for the day. He'd lost a lot of hours taking care of Molly's tires, but he wouldn't have done it any other way. After tossing and turning all night long worrying about her driving on that donut too long, he'd woken up pissed off as normal. There had only been one thing to do.

"You okay, Faust?" Blade asked as he cleaned up his area.

"I'm good."

"Come in and get a beer in a couple of hours," Steele directed.

Faust just nodded and lost himself in the engine repair he was working on. Quiet settled over the shop. He was surprised to find he missed the cacophony that usually filled the space as the guys joked and cursed stubborn repairs. Shaking his head at that thought, Faust moved to the next job he had in line. There were four in front of him.

A honk brought his head up sharply. He waited and listened. There it came again. Walking to the outside door, he picked up a rag to wipe the worst of the oil and lubricants off his hands before grabbing a bat by the cash register.

He flipped the spotlights on to blind anyone outside in the

dark. Bursting through the door, he stopped abruptly at the sight of Molly's car. "Little girl? What are you doing here?"

"I brought you some banana pudding. I had a feeling you missed dinner," Molly said, rushing forward.

"Whoa, Pixie!" Faust stabilized her with his forearms, trying to keep her clothes free of the gunk that coated his hands as Molly bobbled the dish she held in her hands. "Are you okay?"

"Yes. Sorry. I'm a bit clumsy."

"What is this?" Faust asked, nodding at the bowl in her hands.

"Banana pudding. It's my grandmother's recipe. I brought some to you for dinner. It has everything you need in it. Fruit, dairy, whipped cream, and vanilla wafers."

"Did you make this for me?" he asked, attempting to rescue the dish, but she pulled it away. Some of the whipped cream was plastered on the plastic wrap covering the concoction underneath.

"I did. It gets better with age. Day three is my personal favorite," Molly answered. "You need to put it on a table."

"You've eaten this so many times you've rated it by day, hmmm?"

"Grandma knew it was my favorite. Would you try it?" she asked, practically dancing against him.

That tested his ability to control his dick. A lot. "Yes. I'll try it."

"Yay!" She cheered and almost dropped the dish again in her enthusiasm. "I brought you a spoon. It's in my pocket." Molly whirled to show him the metal sticking out of her pocket swaddled in napkins.

"Come on, Pixie. How about we put this on my workstation? It's there with the open tool chest. I need to wash my hands, Little girl."

She looked at his grimy fingers and didn't grimace. He relaxed a bit. Nothing pissed him off more than a woman that looked down at him because he worked with his hands. Well, that's at least in the top ten. He couldn't imagine anything Molly did that would make him angry.

Quickly, he scrubbed his hands with the pumice-filled cleanser. Grabbing a paper towel, he turned and dried his hands as he walked back to his bench. Molly had dragged his stool over and was in the process of folding a large paper napkin into something that resembled—something. He couldn't quite tell.

"Come sit down and I'll give you a lesson in banana pudding."

"It's that difficult to eat?" he asked, unable to keep the corners of his mouth from tilting up.

"Oh, yeah. Look, there are layers." Molly lifted the clear bowl to point at the side. "You've got to get everything in one bite. Let me do the first bite for you."

Faust watched her carefully—almost surgically—scoop out a bite with the large spoon. She raised it to his lips, watching him carefully. What else could he do? Opening his mouth, he allowed the endearing woman to feed him. He didn't care that she smeared a bunch as she completed her self-appointed task.

"Oops!"

Flavor burst over his taste buds. His eyebrows raised as he chewed the concoction. Her face revealed her concern. He realized it was important to her that he loved this. Thank goodness this was the best thing he'd ever eaten.

Swallowing the bite, he licked his lips to remove the traces of the enthusiastic helping she'd spooned into his mouth. "There's only one thing that would make this better, Little girl."

"Oh, no! What?"

"Licking this off your body would be better," Faust told her and watched her eyes widen in surprise.

"Do people do that? With banana pudding?" she whispered.

"I don't care if anyone else does. It's at the top of my to-do list now."

Reaching toward the bowl, he scooped up a small amount of the sweet mixture and spread it on her lips. Faust loved seeing her eyes roll up in pleasure at the sensuous move before her gaze darted back to him, obviously not wishing to miss a second of this. Wrapping his hands around her upper arms, he gently pulled her forward until Molly stood between his legs.

Leaning forward, Faust nibbled at her bottom lip. Her sweet moan went straight to his cock. He swirled his tongue over his current target and felt her hands clamp over his shoulders as if she needed to hold on for stability. Moving to her upper lip, Faust continued savoring the treat.

Her arms wrapped around his neck as she pressed her mouth fully against his. To reward her response, Faust teased her inner lips with his tongue and deepened the kiss as she responded to his unspoken request. The sweet flavor he found inside completely erased the allure of the banana pudding. He pulled her closer, needing to feel her against him.

Flickering lights drew his attention, and Faust lifted his head. Immediately, he realized they were not alone. Lifting Molly off her feet, he stood and carefully set her behind him. A cluster of Shadowridge Guardians stood in the entrance of the garage. He watched them shift weapons away as Molly peeked around him.

"The alarm went off on the door," Steele explained, pointing to the open passage where Faust had let Molly inside.

Faust looked up at the ceiling, inwardly kicking himself. "We're fine."

"Good," Kade said before dabbing at the corner of his mouth. "You've got a little something right here."

"Fuck off," Faust growled and watched the men's amusement.

"Faust, that's not nice," Molly said, sliding around him to wave at the gathered men. "Hi! My fault. I brought Faust some banana pudding as a thank you for helping with my tires."

"Ooo, my nana used to make that," Talon shared.

"Would you like…"

Faust cut in to stop her. "Mine," he stated in a tone that everyone recognized as nonnegotiable.

That sparked additional laughter. Small hands wrapped around one of his arms, hugging it to her body before her hand slid into his. Faust looked down at Molly to see if she was appalled that he wouldn't share. To his delight, she looked happy.

"I'll make more for you all," she promised. "I made this batch for Faust. It's the first time he's had banana pudding. I think he likes it."

"I'd say," Steele agreed with a shit-eating grin. "Come on, guys. Everything is okay here."

"Hey, how did you get to the shop?" Kade asked Molly.

"I just pushed the metal gate open. It wasn't locked," Molly said, tightening her grip on Faust's hand. "I'm sorry. Did I screw something up?"

Giving her a reassuring squeeze, Faust assured her, "You're fine. Someone didn't get the gate secured correctly."

Steele's face hardened and he exchanged a look with Kade. The two men would figure out who didn't do their job correctly. Not only were there a large number of expensive bikes parked in the lot, but the amount of equipment housed in the shop was vast as well. No one should be stupid enough to try to rob the Shadowridge Guardians, but if given the opportunity, someone would take advantage.

"Is she staying?" Kade asked Faust.

"Not long," Faust answered. His Little girl was not ready for him to take her to bed. That kiss had been sweet but tentative. Her experience was limited.

"I can go now," Molly offered nervously.

"No rush," Steele told her before looking at Faust. "You'll lock everything up?"

Faust nodded.

"Let's go. The Li… girls will be scared when we're out here for so long." Kade corrected himself from saying something as he opened the door for everyone.

In a minute they were gone, and the shop was quiet. When

Faust turned to face Molly, she grinned and reached up to wipe away the pudding at the corner of his lips. That grin disappeared when he trapped her hand and guided her finger into his mouth.

He loved the undisguised passion on her face as he swirled his tongue around her index finger. She shimmied closer and pressed a hand to his chest. Faust controlled his desire to sweep everything off his workstation to make love to her. A second plan popped into his head, and he pushed away the idea he could scoop her up and carry her through the clubhouse to his apartment.

He gently pulled her hand away from his face, releasing her digit with a small pop. "Little girl, thank you for the banana pudding."

"You're welcome," she answered politely in a rough voice.

"I'm going to send you home. I'll see you after work tomorrow."

"Oh. You probably have a billion things to do and I'm interrupting." Molly immediately stepped away from him.

"If I keep you here, I'm going to devour a lot of that pudding," he told her, holding her gaze with his.

"Oh!" she repeated and turned a cute shade of pink.

"You're not ready for that. Perhaps on the third day..." He allowed that suggestion to trail away.

"Oh! I should go," she said quickly. "Eat more pudding and then put it in the refrigerator. You have to eat it with that spoon. It makes it taste the best."

"Let's get you in your car."

Faust accompanied her outside and opened her door. When she was safely inside, he leaned in, crowding her against the seat as he fastened her seatbelt. His hand adjusted the strap across her torso, allowing the back of his fingers to brush lightly over her small breasts. Her quick intake of breath told him she'd enjoyed his touch.

"Thank you for the banana pudding, Pixie. Drive safely home and text me when you're safe inside your apartment."

"Okay. Faust…"

He pressed his lips to hers in a light kiss, cutting off her words. When he lifted his head, Faust told her, "Start practicing calling me Daddy."

"Daddy?" she repeated, wide-eyed.

He rewarded her with another kiss before telling her, "Drive carefully."

Forcing himself to stand up, Faust stepped back to close her door and watched her fumble around to start her car. He liked knowing she was affected by his kisses. He walked to the open gate to close it after her.

To his delight, she pulled into the drive and stopped to throw him a kiss before heading through the gate and onto the road. Faust caught himself waving and shook his head as she disappeared over a hill. He had it bad.

After closing the gate, he looked at the lock. It was dark out here, but he couldn't see any marks indicating someone had messed with it. Someone had just fucked up and not secured it. A stickler for safety, Faust's usual anger was lessened by his Little's visit.

Returning to the shop, he closed and locked the door, tucking the bat he'd thrown away back into its spot by the register. Striding toward his work area, Faust picked up the big metal spoon laying amid his tools. He ate several bites before forcing himself to stop.

Faust recovered the bowl. Carrying it and the spoon, he crossed into the clubhouse. He flipped off everyone who inquired about the dish, teasing him about the Little's visit.

"Stop that." Ivy raised her voice to be heard. "I'm glad Faust found his Little and I can't wait to meet her."

Carlee hooked her arm with Ivy and said, "Ditto."

One by one, all the Littles made an adorable chain. Each looked determined.

"Thank you, Littles," Faust said, keeping his expression serious.

"No ribbing Faust about his Little," Atlas proposed, and Carlee ran over to reward him with a kiss.

The other Littles looked expectantly at their Daddies. One by one, they promised, and the chain dwindled until only Ivy remained. Steele walked over to pick her up and toss her over his shoulder.

As she squealed in surprise, Steele spanked her bottom to get her attention before announcing, "I need more convincing."

Everyone hooted and cheered as he carried his Little toward his apartment. The amusement increased when Ivy reached down to deliberately squeeze one of his muscular buns.

Faust followed them down the hall, passing the couple as they walked through their door. He controlled his expression at their playful conversation until he'd reached his apartment. Grinning as he placed the bowl in his fridge with the spoon carefully balanced on top, Faust decided he'd smiled more in the two days he'd known Molly than he'd ever done in his life.

On his way back to work, he stopped to lock his apartment door for the first time since he'd moved in. Those fuckers would go eat his banana pudding. He didn't want to waste time he could spend with Molly beating their asses.

The revelry had resumed in the main room. The Littles were playing a board game at one of the large tables. The guys were scattered in groups around with some clustered at the bar. Faust didn't allow himself to join them. He headed for the door that would take him back to the shop.

"Need help, Faust?" Blade called.

"I've got this." Faust answered. He always worked better by himself anyway. A picture of Molly's sweet face popped into his mind. Maybe alone didn't appeal as much.

CHAPTER
SIX

Molly rubbed her eyes before trying to force them open. If only that alarm clock hadn't rung. She was having the best dream about a tall, tattooed biker.

Finally, she rolled over to turn off the incessant ringing of the alarm. Swinging her legs out of the covers, she pushed herself to sit up. Her gaze landed on the cracked open drawer of her nightstand. She pushed it totally closed, hiding the pink vibrator she'd ordered by mail.

She'd wanted one forever but was too chicken to walk into the adult store in town. Thank goodness she'd noticed the small check box that offered discreet packaging. If they'd just slapped a label on the box, her mailman would have looked at her funny forever.

Dashing into the restroom, she started getting ready for work. In a short time, she stood in her kitchen debating if she wanted one cup of coffee or if she should make a pot. Limiting herself to one, she grabbed one of the bananas that hadn't made it into the pudding.

In just a few minutes, she finished her coffee as she stood, checking through her email. Clearing out her mailbox, Molly left a few to check out later. After rinsing her cup, she grabbed her purse and a box of crackers. Taking the pudding to Faust had wiped out the time when she prepared her lunch. Crackers would give her something to munch on. Besides, she was going to dinner with Faust—that was a treat.

Molly dashed into her closet to grab shoes to match the dress she wore. She lingered for just a minute, scanning her clothes hoping for something exciting to wear on her date. Everything she had screamed church secretary. Giving up, she stepped into a pair of sandals and headed for the door.

The trip to the church was quick and Molly pulled into the parking spot she usually took. Once inside, Molly navigated to the office and automatically moved through her morning routine. When she sat down at her desk, she saw the message light blinking once again. Crossing her fingers that everything was okay, she hit the play button. Fortunately, they were all simple to resolve.

Breathing a sigh of relief, Molly sat back in her chair and started working on the letters Minister Steve had requested. She greeted the two men as they entered at different times. The day seemed so normal compared to yesterday. She found herself wishing for a little excitement and pushed that desire away. It was better to have boring normalcy in the office.

I'll get my excitement later.

She squirmed a bit on her chair, thinking about the tall, muscular biker. He was so totally different from anyone she knew. Was she dating him only because he was a bad boy? For the excitement?

"I see something in him no one else does."

"Your biker?" Minister Steve said as he walked toward her desk.

"Oh, I'm sorry. I didn't mean to say that out loud." Mentally, she struck herself on the forehead.

"Molly, you get to decide who your friends are. I'm going to put one thought into your mind as an old man who's worked with a lot of people. Others will judge you by the company you keep."

"Amen." Lester O'Brien's voice carried down the hall, confirming Molly's suspicion that he could hear everything said in the main office area.

"Thank you, Minister Steve, for caring about me. I'll keep that in mind," Molly answered diplomatically.

"You have a long life ahead of you. Being happy is the most important," Minister Steve added.

Molly nodded.

"And your eternal soul," the assistant minister added from his office.

Minister Steve shook his head and walked down the hallway into Lester's office, closing the door after him.

Molly strained her ears trying to hear their conversation. She did hear Lester's voice raising at times. Minister Steve's even tone reassured her. He always had a positive energy around him. She wondered if the minister considered his assistant to be his personal challenge.

Molly focused on her computer screen when Minister Steve walked back into his office. She worked diligently to clear all the items from her to-do list. By lunch time, she'd made a big dent in her weekly tasks.

Wishing to get up and move a bit, Molly stood and decided to spend a bit of her lunch break outside. She exited to the parking lot and breathed in the fresh air feeling better already. Reaching her hands up to the sky first, she stretched out her back and twisted to each side.

Already she felt better. Walking around the parking lot, the wind ruffled her hair. Molly looked up at the fast-approaching clouds and realized a storm was coming in. She quickened her steps and headed diagonally across the parking lot toward the door to speed up her progress back inside.

The thought crossed her mind that she hoped Faust was

inside. Riding a motorcycle in a storm didn't sound like a good idea.

She'd almost reached the door when a massive gust of wind buffeted her, almost knocking Molly off her feet. As she struggled to regain her balance, the strong breeze swirled around her legs lifting her skirt up to a revealing level. Panicking, she pushed it down and ran forward toward the building.

After darting inside, Molly heard a huge thunderclap of thunder that rocked the building and the skies opened to pour water onto the pavement. She wrapped her arms around herself, shivering after the scary encounter with Mother Nature.

"You should be ashamed of yourself, Molly. What a display in the church parking lot!"

She spun around to see Lester standing behind her. "That storm is awful out there. The wind was uncontrollable."

"Don't make excuses, girl," the unpleasant man answered.

Molly forced herself to keep her mouth closed. Surely he didn't think she'd flapped her dress up to her waist for the sheer pleasure of putting her panties on display. Oh, crap! She'd put on her white underwear with yellow rubber duckies today.

You did nothing wrong.

Repeating that thought over and over in her mind, she headed back to the office. Molly sat down on her chair. Her gaze landed on the adorable stuffie she hadn't been able to leave again. She leaned forward to brush her fingers over Angel's soft fuzz and quickly shifted her hand to pull out the crackers as a woman opened the door.

"Hi, Mrs. Alberts. What can I do for you?"

The woman's gaze landed on the cracker. "I'm sorry, Molly. I didn't mean to disturb your lunch."

"I'm glad to help you."

"I wanted to inquire about helping with communion," the older woman told her.

Noticing the woman's arthritic hands, Molly guessed the heavy communion trays would be too much. She knew immediately who she needed to talk to. "How nice of you to volunteer. Let me check with Minister Steve to see if he has time to talk to you."

"I've got time," answered her as the gentle man's voice carried out of the office.

Smiling, Molly escorted her down the hall. Minister Steve would take care of everything and everyone.

The afternoon flew by. Molly tried to keep from looking at the clock every five minutes. At a quarter to five, she heard her cell phone ring. Grabbing it, she grinned at his name and answered, "Hi."

"Hi, Little girl. I couldn't remember if I was picking you up at the church or your apartment."

"Oh, my apartment would be better." Molly quickly recited the information. "I get off here at 5. I should be there by a quarter after."

"Drive safely. I'll be there when you pull in," Faust promised.

"Okay. I'm looking forward to it. Um…" She hesitated before adding, "I might need to change."

"I'll wait until you're ready."

"Thanks."

"Soon, Little girl. Drive safely home."

"Soon," she echoed, silently adding Daddy to the end of that statement.

Disconnecting, Molly stared at the phone as she tried to pull herself together. How did he have such an effect on her? It wasn't that he represented danger or living on the wild side. He made her happy. Even just hearing his voice made her happy.

When the second hand reached the twelve, Molly jumped up to grab her purse and tote bag. She left her crackers. They could be her lunch tomorrow. She didn't plan to get home early enough to throw anything together.

"Good night!" she called to the men still in their offices and didn't wait for their responses.

Emerging from the church, Molly was tickled to see the rain had passed, and the sun was peeking out of wispy clouds. She almost skipped to her car and slid in behind the steering wheel. In seconds, she had herself organized.

Molly drove carefully home. By the time she pulled into her apartment complex, she was buzzing with excitement. She turned the corner to see her apartment building. Her heart dropped. There wasn't a bike anywhere. He hadn't come to get her.

Instant tears prickled her eyes. Blinking furiously, she pulled into a random parking space. Her usual one held a large pickup with heavily tinted windows. She took a minute to try and pull herself together. Hearing a car door slam, she looked up to see who she'd have to make it past to get to her apartment. Faust stalked forward toward her.

She threw her door open and raced to jump up into his arms. He caught her easily and held her close.

"Now that's a welcome, Pixie," he said with the corners of his mouth twitching upward.

"Were you in that truck? When I didn't see your bike, I thought you'd decided not to come."

"I will never go back on my word, Little girl," he said sternly.

"O—Okay. Sorry."

"Don't apologize for a misunderstanding. I should have warned you. We hadn't talked about riding a bike, so I borrowed Steele's truck."

"I've never ridden on a motorcycle," she confessed.

"That's what I figured. I'll give you some lessons when you're ready to ride on my bike."

"That sounds like fun," she said and laid her head on his shoulder as she tried to blink away her tears. His hand stroked over her back soothing her as if he understood just how upset she had been.

"Are you hungry, Little girl?" he asked.

"Oh, I'm wasting time," she blurted, wiggling to get down.

"Holding you is not wasting time. Ever," he assured her as he set Molly's feet safely on the ground.

She smiled at him, feeling his words all the way to her heart. "I was going to change into jeans to ride on your bike. I've already had my dress blow up today. Zero out of five stars—do not recommend."

"Do I need to kill someone?"

She blinked at his instantly serious look. He was kidding, right? "Um. No one. I just walked around the parking lot and that storm popped it. It whipped my skirt up."

"Would you be more comfortable in jeans?" He didn't address her explanation, but his expression softened once again.

Molly hesitated, feeling the wind still blowing around her. "That's probably smarter."

"Go, Pixie. I'll wait right here."

"Okay. I'll be fast."

Molly turned around to see her driver's door open. She looked over her shoulder to see Faust nod in encouragement. Leaning in, she grabbed her purse and tote bag from the passenger seat before realizing the view she was providing him. Embarrassed, she quickly stood up and slammed the door shut.

She turned to look at him and saw him adjust himself inside those snug jeans. Something inside her heated as Molly recognized she had been the cause of his condition. Hiding her grin until she turned back to the building, Molly hurried inside and up the stairs to her apartment.

Racing to her bedroom, Molly took thirty seconds to tuck Angel safely in bed. "Go to sleep. I'll be home in a bit."

With that task completed, she dashed into her closet and pulled the dress over her head as she slid out of her sensible pumps. After putting one in the laundry bin and the other in her shoe rack, Molly found her favorite pair of jeans and debated on the right shirt.

The image of Faust in his snug black T-shirt popped into her mind. Impulsively, she grabbed her pink shirt with a black accent trim around the neck and sleeves. They'd match without being too obvious.

Quickly pulling on the clothes, she grabbed her favorite pair of sneakers. She only wore them on special occasions to keep them clean. In a few minutes, she had socks and her high-tops on. She took a minute to pee and put a bit of eyeliner, mascara, and tinted lip gloss on.

Returning to the bedroom, she grabbed her purse and waved goodbye to an already sleepy Angel. Molly took time to lock her apartment door before rushing down the stairs and out the door. Faust pushed away from the truck. His face looked panicked as he ran forward.

"Stop!"

Immediately, she skidded to a halt. A car rushed past her the next second. She felt the rush of air as it continued through the apartment complex at a high rate of speed. Shocked, she let her breath out in a long gust.

"Are you okay?" Faust was by her side. He gripped her upper arms while he scanned her body looking for any injury.

"I'm fine. What a doofus I am! He would have splatted me on the pavement," she said, trying to joke off the scare that still had her pulse racing.

"You need your bottom spanked for not looking both ways," Faust stated as his fingers tightened around her arms.

"Ha, ha! Good one, Faust," she said with a cheerful laugh.

"I'm not a comedian, Little girl. Nor do I threaten anything I don't plan to follow through on. Let's go up to your apartment."

"What?" Her heart beat faster for an entirely different reason. He didn't plan on spanking her…Did he?

"Take me to your apartment, Molly."

Swallowing hard, she looked at him. How much did she trust

him? Flashes of their interactions burst across her mind. Faust had taken care of her in every situation.

"I don't want to be spanked," she whispered.

"I don't think anyone wants to be punished," Faust told her. He waited for her to make up her mind.

Molly put her hand in his and pulled him forward. She led him inside and up the stairs to the top floor. She noticed Faust was never out of breath while she panted slightly. Stopping outside apartment 403, Molly dug her keys out of her purse and opened the door.

Leading the way inside, she watched Faust look around as if checking for security. She closed the door and leaned against it, waiting to see what he would do. When he turned around and walked forward to cage her against the door, Molly dropped her purse to the ground, forgetting it completely as he kissed her.

Clinging to his body, Molly was swept away by the passion and emotion in his kiss. She could feel his concern and relief as he explored her mouth with a dominance that made her heart beat so fast. When he ripped his mouth away from hers, she stared up at his fierce face.

"I'm sorry," she whispered.

"I'm sorry, Daddy," he corrected her.

"I'm sorry, Daddy," she repeated, feeling the importance of that word on her mind and body. It felt like the link between them closed. She stepped forward to close the distance between them, lifting her mouth in silent supplication.

Faust cupped the back of her head as he lowered his lips to hers. This kiss was as sweet as the other had been fierce and demanding. Her heart fluttered in her chest as she wrapped her arms around his neck. Taking his time, he tasted her as if she were the finest wine in the world.

When she touched her tongue to his, Faust rewarded her by stroking his hands down her spine to cup her bottom, lifting her to align their bodies perfectly. She shivered against him at the feel of his thick shaft pressing against her. A soft moan escaped her when shown that he wanted her, Molly Abrams.

Molly had never been so tuned on. She'd kissed boys in high school but had never felt anything like this. How did he create such a fire inside her?

She gripped him tightly when he lifted his head to end the kiss. He's not going to stop, is he? Molly held her breath as he walked over to her worn couch. Without any awkwardness, Faust maneuvered her legs to the side and sat down with her cuddled on his lap.

"Little girl. You took ten years off my life and added a few gray hairs."

Molly couldn't help looking up at his bald head. Gray hair? When her gaze met his once again, she couldn't help but giggle at the amusement on his normally scowling face.

"Are you laughing at your Daddy?" he asked.

"No!" she promised, trying to control her amusement.

"That's my Little girl. Now, you weren't such a good girl a few minutes ago."

"I didn't mean to scare you. I stopped when you yelled."

"You did. You also endangered yourself by not looking both ways. Next time, I will come to the other side to walk with you."

"Are you going to spank me?" she whispered.

"Yes. I want you to remember to be safe whether you're excited or not."

"But..."

"There are no buts. Come stand in front of Daddy," Faust directed. He stood her between his legs and unfastened her jeans.

Freezing at the feel of his hands, she couldn't react until his hands tugged the material over her hips. She twisted to each side, but Faust didn't allow her to escape. He held her securely in place as he continued to draw the thick material down.

"I'll let you wear panties this time. Next time you endanger yourself, I will strip your bottom bare."

When she caught herself nodding, Molly switched to turn her head back and forth.

"Daddy is always in charge, Little girl. It's easier on your bottom to agree."

Before she could argue with that, he lifted her easily and draped her body over his muscular thighs. Holding onto his calf for balance, she marveled at the sheer size of his muscles. He had to weight lift.

His first swat made the question in her mind about his exercise regimen evaporate. "Hey! That hurt!"

"It's supposed to hurt," he assured her as he delivered two more stinging spanks.

"Ow! No more. I'm sorry." Her bottom stung already.

"I'll know when you've had enough," he told her as he continued to pepper her bottom.

Heat built in her tender skin as he punished her. Molly sagged over his lap as her fight vanished. He was in charge. She'd almost gotten hit. She could have missed any future with him. Heartsick from that thought, Molly felt tears drip from her eyes. She drew a ragged breath as she tried unsuccessfully not to sob.

"Have you learned your lesson, Little girl?" he asked.

"Yes! I could... I could have messed up us," she pushed out.

His hand smoothed over her red skin. "And hurt yourself badly. That would have made my sunny disposition unpleasant."

The thought of the aggressive man becoming unpleasant made her hug his leg tight. "I promise. I'll look both ways."

"That's my good girl."

The world whirled around her once again as he lifted her to sit on his lap. She gasped as her stinging bottom landed on his denim-clad, hard thigh. Her gaze flew to meet his.

"Spankings are supposed to hurt, Little girl. Your bottom will remind you to be careful for some time."

"Are you always going to spank me?" she blurted.

"No. Spankings are effective ways to get your attention and change your behavior. There are other ways to correct you."

"Like what?" she whispered, half in fascination, half in dismay.

"You could have to write lines, sit in the corner, lose something important to you for a period of time, not get to wear panties under your dress... There are a million punishments."

As she stared at him not sure what to say, he added, "I could even add extras to punishments like holding your vibrator to your wet pussy as your stand in the corner."

"You wouldn't do that!" she said shocked.

"Try me."

Molly wasn't about to do that.

When she didn't answer, he grabbed a couple of tissues and held them to her nose. "Blow."

"I can do it!" she rushed to tell him in embarrassment.

"Daddy's got it," he said, not allowing her to take them from him.

After a short hesitation, Molly exhaled delicately through her nose.

"Blow, Pixie."

This time, she blew her nose as if she held the tissues to her nose. He expertly wiped her nose and crumpled the layers in his hand. Dropping that on the floor, he grabbed a few more to wipe her face free of tears.

Her stomach growled loudly as he took care of her.

"Sounds like we need to feed you, Little girl. Tonight is taco night at the Shadowridge Guardians' clubhouse. Would you like to go there or out to a restaurant?"

"Are the other Littles going to be there?"

"I'm sure there will be several. You can stay with me after we eat, or you can play with them."

"You," Molly said quickly. She didn't have a lot of close friends. It seemed scary to talk to others who had Daddies. Maybe they'd decide she wasn't really Little.

"I'd like that, too, Pixie." He leaned in to kiss her before standing her between his legs. "Turn around, Little girl. Let me see your bottom."

Without thinking, she whirled around. She squealed in protest as he hooked a finger into her panties to pull down the back. He controlled her impulse to dart away as he looked over her bottom. His hand smoothed over her skin.

"Be still. I need to see how you took your punishment. It looks like your bottom survived well. That's good to know for the future."

She stared at his bald head as he turned her back to face him and drew up the material. When her jeans were fastened, he asked her gently, "Are you ready to go or do you need to potty?"

"Let me fix my makeup. I must look awful."

"You look adorable, but I'll wait a few minutes. Go on, Little girl. You have three minutes."

She darted away as he looked at his watch.

CHAPTER
SEVEN

After turning into the Shadowridge compound, Faust reached over the console to wrap his hand around her thigh. He squeezed slightly. Immediately, her squirming stopped. "People are going to love you, Molly. You've already met several of them."

"I don't know their names."

"That's okay. They don't know your name, either."

He lifted his hand to turn the steering wheel as he parked then replaced it to hold her in place. "Stay where you are until I help you out."

"I'm not going to play in traffic," she promised, sounding a bit exasperated.

"Daddy will open your door. You will stay there." He let that statement fade out in the posh interior.

"Okay," she whispered.

Faust knew she'd figured out there was an implied punishment that would follow if she didn't choose wisely. "Thank you, Pixie."

Sliding from the cab, he scanned the parking lot to see who was at the clubhouse. There were two helmets on several bikes. He nodded, inwardly pleased that there would be Littles to make Molly feel at home. Faust opened her door and plucked his Little from the cab.

He drew her close and let her brush his body as he lowered her to the ground. Her quiet gasp pleased him. Making love to Molly would be explosive. She was so responsive.

When she stumbled, visibly affected by their contact, he took her hand and led her to the back of the truck. "Here's a traffic crossing. What do you do?" he asked.

"Look left and right." She followed what they had practiced on the way. "There's no one here, Daddy. It's a parking lot."

"Ahem."

"Oh, yeah. Right. I'll try again."

This time after she'd checked for traffic, he allowed her to tug him forward. He led her to the door and squeezed her hand. "If at any time you feel uncomfortable, let me know and we'll leave."

"Really?"

"Absolutely."

When she smiled, Faust opened the door and walked in first to check out the clubhouse. Molly walked in right behind him as if glued to his body. He gave her hand another squeeze.

"Faust!" Several club members shouted his name to welcome him.

"This is Molly. She's mine," Faust declared.

"Hi, Molly," the members greeted her.

He saw a movement to the left catch Molly's attention. Three women poked their heads out from under the edge of a blanket draped over the furniture. They'd made a fort. That's fun.

Faust watched Molly's reaction and loved the wide smile as she returned their greeting wave before Carlee called, "Come join us, Molly."

He knew she wasn't quite ready to leave him yet. "She needs to eat first. Then I'll see if she wants to play," Faust answered for her and felt her squeeze his hand in a silent thanks.

"How many tacos can you eat, Molly? I bet three," a man asked from behind the kitchen island.

"That's Gabriel. He's an amazing cook," Faust explained.

"Hi, Gabriel. Could I have two?" Molly asked politely.

"You can. Chicken, beef, or one of each?" Gabriel asked as he grabbed a plate.

"One of each."

Gabriel held out a plate to lure her forward. "Come put all the toppings on that you like while I dish up ten tacos for your Daddy."

"Ten tacos?" she repeated in wonder.

"That will be a good start," Faust answered.

He watched her take her plate and survey all the things she could add to her tacos. The Shadowridge Guardians didn't skimp on taco night. There was a huge array of choices as well as rice and beans to top everything off. Molly skipped the jalapenos and added sour cream, cheddar cheese, lettuce, and salsa. Faust approved of all those choices.

"Put a bit of the corn salsa on your plate to try," he suggested.

Molly nodded and put a small pile on her plate. She added a bit of rice and beans to finish off her choices. When she returned to hover close to him, Faust rubbed her back quickly before finishing his selections. Placing his hand on her lower back, he guided her to a partially filled table that included Blade, Kade, and Steele.

"You all remember Molly, right?" he said to remind them of her name.

"Of course," Blade said. "He still hasn't shared his banana pudding, Molly."

"Oh. I guess I should have made some for everyone," she rushed to say.

"Maybe you'd share your recipe with me one evening? It's obviously the best thing ever," Gabriel said, setting a plastic glass in front of her that was topped with a lid. He gave Faust a glass of cola.

"Thanks, Gabriel."

"I figured you were driving a special passenger," Gabriel commented.

"Exactly," Faust said, setting a possessive hand on Molly's slim thigh. "Eat, Pixie. Don't let your food get cold."

He watched her pick up a taco and take a small bite. Her expressive face revealed her delight as she chewed quickly to eat more. "Gabriel has a special touch with tacos. Everyone likes them."

"Even your Daddy and he doesn't like anything," Blade joked.

"He likes me," Molly stated firmly, standing up for her Daddy.

"He does. I guess I can't say that anymore," Blade agreed.

"Nope," Molly said cheerfully before trying the rice and groaning at the delicious taste.

She didn't hold a grudge at all. Faust could tell Blade was immediately forgiven for his mistake. Even in a situation she wasn't comfortable in, Molly hadn't let someone speak poorly of him. Faust knew Blade always had his back. The weapon expert had just made a joke.

Faust was used to everyone expecting the worst from him. He definitely didn't approach others with a smile and an open heart. His actions convinced everyone to notice his hot temper that was quick to respond to any slight. If others were frightened by him, that was okay in Faust's view.

"How about tomorrow afternoon to look at your engine?" Faust suggested.

"I can wait until you're caught up," Blade assured him.

"Tomorrow afternoon," Faust repeated.

"Perfect." Blade agreed with his rigid suggestion.

"Do you always work on engines?" Molly asked as she poked her fork at the corn salsa he'd told her to put on her plate.

"Blade's good at everything but he has a magical touch with engines," Steele said. "Mine is running smoother than it did straight off the assembly line."

A woman appeared next to Steele, and he wrapped his arm around her waist to pick her up. He set her gently on his lap before leaning down to press a kiss to her lips.

"Did you get tired of the blanket fort?" he asked.

"No. I wanted to get to know Molly better. I also thought I could eat one more taco," Ivy answered.

"Let's see." Steele gently poked her tummy in three different places. "There's enough room in there for two tacos."

Ivy laughed. Her delighted giggle made everyone around smile.

"Here you go, Little girl," Gabriel said, placing a plate with two tacos on it in front of her.

"I can't eat both of those," Ivy protested.

"You won't have to. Eden's on her way over to help you," Gabriel said, nodding at his Little girl who approached.

"Oh, good." Ivy smiled at Molly. "Hi, Molly. I'm Ivy."

"Hi, Ivy," Molly said and wiggled a bit closer to Faust.

He wrapped his arm over the top of her chair and hugged her to him reassuringly. "The motorcycle club has officers that guide the actions of the group. Steele was chosen to be the President. He's Ivy's Daddy."

"So, you're like the head of the Littles group?" Molly whispered.

"Oh, no. We don't have any leaders. We just have fun," Ivy reassured her as the other woman sat down.

Gabriel placed an empty plate in front of her and two similar cups in front of each Little. "Ivy would like you to eat one of her tacos. Could you help her out?"

"Sure, Daddy," Eden said with a smile at the handsome man taking care of the kitchen before scooping up the nearest taco. "Mmm. Just how I like them."

"A little birdie gave me the inside scoop," Gabriel said before dropping a kiss on her head and wandering off.

"I'm Eden, Molly. I'm glad to meet you." The new arrival waved her taco Molly's way and added, "My Daddy makes the best tacos."

"Hi. They're delicious. If Ivy's Daddy is the president, is your Daddy the Vice President?" Molly asked.

"Nope. That's Storm." She turned and pointed to a bearded man with tattoos covering his muscular arms. "Gabriel is the Chaplain."

"So, he's a minister?" Molly asked, leaning forward.

"Not like a church minister who gives a sermon on Sunday. Gabriel supports everyone. A lot of people come to him to talk about things. He does fun activities like taco night to get everyone together," Eden said. "He and Bear feed us a lot. Everyone loves when he makes food."

"Everything is amazing," Molly said and took another bite.

The other women followed suit and they all munched happily for a minute as Faust methodically devoured the ones on his plate. He knew Molly watched him out of the corner of her eye.

"The record for number of tacos eaten at one meal is twenty-seven," Ivy whispered.

"Who ate that many?" Molly asked.

"Me. I was hungry," Blade volunteered.

Molly looked at Faust and he shook his head. "I'd have to run miles to work those off." He rubbed his hand over his abdomen and stifled a groan as Molly's gaze followed his movement before shifting a bit lower.

She is going to be the death of me. Faust clamped down on his control. He didn't need to get a hardon at the table.

"Drink some milk, Pixie," he suggested, and her gaze zipped up to meet his. Her cheeks turned pink as she realized he'd caught her ogling him. Quickly, she picked up the cup and drank deeply.

"I like that. Pixie. My Daddy calls me Ladybug," Eden shared.

When Molly looked over at Ivy, she answered the unspoken question. "I'm Little girl," Ivy offered.

"Does everyone have a Little girl?" Molly whispered.

"Not everyone is so lucky," Blade answered.

"She's out there, Blade. You just need to find her. We thought Faust would be the last one..." Ivy's voice drifted off as if she felt she'd stuck her foot in her mouth.

Faust snorted and took another bite. It didn't bother him at all to have the others skeptical that he could attract someone as special as a Little girl. He couldn't believe his luck, either.

"What do you mean? Why would Faust have trouble finding his Little girl?" Molly demanded in a defensive tone Faust had never heard from her.

"Unruffle your feathers, Pixie. They didn't mean anything bad."

"Oh, no! The minute that came out of my mouth I knew I'd said that wrong. Sorry. Faust would protect any of the Shadowridge Guardians and their Littles until his last breath." Ivy rushed to smooth over her blunder.

"Definitely." Eden backed her up.

"Does anyone feel like playing Simon Says?" Faust asked to distract everyone.

"Could we? You'll be Simon?" Eden asked.

"I'll be Simon," he agreed.

"Faust is the best Simon. No one can ever tell from his expression if he's trying to get you out," Ivy shared.

"And he's so fast. No one can think that quickly," Eden said. She took the last bite of her taco and looked over at Ivy. "Are you finished? We could go move everything out of the way."

"I'm done!" Ivy agreed.

The two women stood up and picked up their dishes. Molly surprised Faust by standing as well. "Can I come help? I can't eat another bite."

"Of course. Come on. We'll introduce you to everyone," Eden answered with a smile.

The three reached the sink and Faust knew Ivy and Eden were explaining they could only carry their plate to the sink. He watched Ivy say something to Molly. When the two hugged, he knew Ivy had apologized again. Eden threw her arms around them both and they swayed for a second together.

"I wasn't expecting Molly to join them," Blade said, turning in his chair to see what happened.

"She's full of surprises," Faust acknowledged.

Faust stood at the front of a cleared area. The Little girls had formed a line in front of him. He stared them all down and heard their giggles. Pleased to see his Little standing between Eden and Ivy, he knew she was acclimating to the group.

When the tension had built, he barked orders.

"Simon says, take a step back."

"Simon says, hop twice."

"Simon says, turn in a circle."

"Turn again."

He paused and one Little caught herself in the middle of a twirl. "Carlee, you're out."

"Simon says, belch."

That one made everyone laugh in the audience as the Littles tried to follow his orders. Molly let loose a loud one that made everyone freeze. Faust clapped and everyone joined him, turning her embarrassment into giggles.

"Simon says, quack like a duck."

"Simon says, walk like a duck."

"Flap your wings like a duck."

"Ivy, you're out."

"Oh, man!" Ivy walked over to join her Daddy who gave her a consolation kiss to cheer her up.

In the next round, Adelaine and Elizabeth slithered like a snake when they shouldn't have and were eliminated. They were followed immediately by Harper who took a giant step forward while everyone else stood still. She whacked herself playfully on the forehead and moved to the side to sit with Carlee and the others.

Only two remained: Remi and Molly. Faust watched the two Littles look at each other assessing their competition. He ran through five Simon says commands in rapid succession before saying, "Sit down."

Remi dropped to the floor followed a split second later by Molly. He could tell by the look on her face that his Little had thrown herself out so Remi wouldn't be upset.

"You're both out! I win," Faust declared, holding his arms up over his head as the victor.

"Blanket fort," Carlee called and linked her elbow with Molly. "You'll come with us?"

"If you'd like," Molly agreed.

"Of course. You're one of us now," Carlee told her.

Molly looked back at Faust and waved before crawling into the blanket fort. He loved the smile on her face. When everyone was inside, he could hear giggles and laughter. Exclamations of delight abounded when Gabriel slid a plate of warm cookies on a skateboard into the opening.

"It's a good feeling, isn't it, big guy?" Atlas asked, whacking him on the back. "Good game. They love it when you call for them."

"It is a good feeling," Faust agreed. He turned down the beer he was offered at the bar. He wanted to be fully able to drive Molly home safely.

CHAPTER
EIGHT

She held Faust's hand as they walked up the flights of stairs to her apartment. Covering her mouth with her hand as she yawned, Molly knew she'd need a big cup of coffee for work tomorrow.

"You're exhausted, Pixie."

"I had so much fun. The other Littles are wonderful."

"They are special."

Molly peeked at him from the corner of her eye. "Did you want any of them to be your Little?"

"Hell, no."

"Why not?" Molly had to ask.

"Each of the Littles are perfect for their Daddies. They wouldn't be happy with me, and I wouldn't be happy with them."

"You think I'm the one you've been looking for?"

"No. I know you're the one I've searched to find. You've just been hiding in a church office."

"You could go to church," Molly assured him. "You know. If you wanted to."

"I tend to make people uncomfortable. People go to hear a minister help them grow or feel better—not to feel like they're going to be robbed," Faust told her as he took the keys from her hand to open her door.

"They wouldn't think that," Molly assured him, but knew some probably would. Maybe if he was with her?

"You, Pixie, always look at people in the best light. I always see the worst. Maybe that's why we fit so good together." Faust lifted Molly off her feet and pressed her against the wall. His kiss took her breath away.

"Go inside and go to bed. No play time with your toys," he said, giving her a look that told her he knew everything about her plans.

"Party pooper." Molly popped her hand over her mouth, realizing she'd just called him a name and confirmed she planned to play after he left.

"I've been called much worse. Your pleasure now happens with me. Not in your bedroom alone."

"That's not fair. You're not the boss of me."

Faust raised one eyebrow and looked at her. "You always have choice, Pixie. It just comes with consequences."

"How will you know?" she asked.

"Go get your vibrator and bring it to me."

"What?"

"I'm protecting the bottom of a Little girl who is already planning to need punishment again," he told her solemnly.

"Faust," she hissed, looking down the hall to make sure no one was outside her apartment.

He simply held out his hand. She stared him down. His unrelenting face didn't give her any hope. He'd stand there until she caved. In less than thirty seconds, she said, "Fine."

Disappearing into her apartment, Molly started to stomp her feet but didn't want to wake up the people below her. Walking without the loud statement didn't feel as satisfying even if she was thinking mean thoughts as she went into her bedroom and opened her nightstand. When she turned around, Faust stood in the bedroom doorway.

"Oh!" she said, startled.

"I decided that if you're being bratty, you must be too tired to get ready for bed by yourself."

"I can do it," Molly answered, propping one hip against the bed as she yawned widely. His suggestion had zapped the last of her ability to hide the exhaustion draped over her like a heavy blanket.

"Where's your nightgown, Pixie?" Faust asked, taking her vibrator from her hand and sticking it in his back pocket.

"Under my pillow."

He reached around her to tug it free and draped it over his shoulder before pulling the covers down. She looked longingly at the sheets and started to climb into bed.

"Not yet, Little girl."

He lifted her back to stand in front of him. Faust knelt in front of her and removed her shoes and socks. When his fingers unfastened her jeans, she rested a hand on his shoulder for balance. Her eyes kept drifting shut. She felt him draw her underwear and pants down her legs and thought of being embarrassed but didn't have the energy for it.

Her hands drifted over his hard body when he stood. "You work out a lot, don't you, Daddy?" she mumbled.

"Yes."

She waited for him to say more but he simply removed her shirt and bra before pulling her nightshirt over her head. Molly threw her arms around his neck when he picked her up. Carrying her into the bathroom, he set Molly on her feet.

"Go potty."

Without thinking, she sat down to pee as he put toothpaste on her toothbrush. "We matched today, Daddy," she mumbled.

"I noticed. You made me look good tonight," he answered as he gathered some toilet paper and handed it to her.

"I need to take a shower," she insisted as she stood up to flush the toilet. "And you already look scrumptious."

"Shower tomorrow morning. And scrumptious?"

"Mmm. Definitely." She picked up the toothbrush and scrubbed it around her mouth for a few seconds before proclaiming, "Done."

"Not done. You only brushed three teeth." Faust took it from her hand and held it to her lips until she opened her mouth. He expertly brushed her teeth.

"That feels good," she mumbled around the brush.

"Here's some water. Rinse your mouth, Little girl."

When she'd accomplished that task, he wrapped an arm around her waist and guided her back to the bedroom. "Oh!" she gasped as he scooped her up in his strong arms and placed her on the bed.

"I need Angel," she insisted.

"She's right here, Pixie." Faust tucked the teddy bear into her arms. Instantly relaxing, she closed her eyes as he tucked the covers under her chin.

Hugging Angel against her body, Molly whispered, "Night-night kiss, Daddy."

Faust pressed his lips to hers and kissed her slowly. The exchange was sweet but intense. Molly didn't have any doubt that Faust was staking his claim and she loved it. No one had ever cared enough about her to want her to know she belonged to him.

"Mmm!" She hummed when he stood up.

"Go to sleep, Little girl. We'll talk tomorrow."

"Night, Daddy."

Waking up the next morning, Molly blinked her eyes open and looked around. She still held Angel and it seemed like she hadn't moved at all. After checking the time, she relaxed against the pillow for a few seconds to remember the previous evening.

"Oh, goodness. He saw me naked," Molly realized.

It had been embarrassing for him to see her bottom covered by her underwear. Now, he'd seen her naked and not even with the distraction of sex. Okay, maybe sex isn't a distraction. The thought of doing it with Faust made her squirm. She hadn't even seen him without his shirt and knew he'd look good.

Faust as a lover? Molly fanned herself. He would be intense. She'd only had a one-night stand, but she'd seen lots of seductions on TV and in the movies. Faust would be way dreamier than those guys.

She reached out a hand from under the covers to grab her vibrator and remembered. Faust had put it in his back pocket. He hadn't walked out the door with that there. Had he? Molly would never be able to meet her neighbors' eyes.

Forcing herself out of bed on that cheery thought, she went to shower before work. Stepping under the spray before it got fully warm, Molly felt the last of her tiredness evaporate. She'd had such a good time at the Shadowridge Guardians' clubhouse. It had been fun to spend time with her Daddy and the Littles.

Catching sight of the time, she hurried and threw on a dress and shoes before racing out of the house. Her crackers would do for lunch again today. She admired her new tires as she approached her car. While it was so nice he had purchased them for her, it was even more important that he wanted her to be safe —whether he was her Daddy or not. Isn't that what a Daddy would do?

Driving the familiar route to work, Molly was lost in thought. Where did they go from here? Would he be interested in her in a month? A year? He was so hunky. And she was just herself.

Molly tried to push her thoughts away as she pulled into the parking lot. The two ministers were already there. She was still early—just not there to open the building for them. After parking, she hurried across the lot and into the church.

"Good morning," Molly called as she settled in her chair.

"Good morning, Molly," Minister Steve answered.

"There's no coffee," Lester shared.

"On it. I'll bring you a cup in a few minutes."

Molly turned on her computer first before quickly setting up the machine and hitting brew. Inwardly, she rolled her eyes that Lester hadn't started it for them. It wasn't rocket science.

She listened to the messages left on the phone, making a stack for each minister before brewing two cups of coffee and walking down the hall. There was one message that was blank— just a recording of several seconds. She figured it was a butt call from someone in the congregation.

"You didn't have to bring me a cup, but thank you," Minister Steve said as he looked up from the spiral notebook where he always wrote his sermons' first drafts.

"My pleasure. Here are a couple of calls I thought you'd wish to address," Molly shared, handing him the notes she'd gotten from the messages.

"On it. Thanks, Molly."

Continuing down the hall, she plastered a smile on her face before walking through the door. "Hi, Lester. Coffee as promised. Here are your messages."

He looked over the list. "Lawncare, teen outing, and new hymnals? I don't think I need to deal with these. Just take care of them." He thrust the sheet back at her.

"Sorry, Lester. Those decisions have to be made by one of the clergy." Molly set the page down on the corner of his desk and walked out before he could give her a title in name only.

There was a message on her phone when she got back to her desk. She was tickled to see it was Faust making sure she got to work safely and had slept well. Molly sent him a return message and forced herself to get to work.

CHAPTER
NINE

"Hi!" Molly chirped as she opened her apartment door that evening. "Did you put googly eyes on my mailbox last night before you left? I laughed so hard when I found them when I got home."

After kissing her hard, Faust held her tightly against him as he walked into her space. He closed the door behind him before looking down at her sweet face. "Googly eyes? What are those?"

"You know. The funny eyes that have pupils that move. They come in stickers that you can place on anything to make it look like a person. It was funny on my mailbox."

"That wasn't me, Little girl. Did you leave them there?" he asked.

"No. They were so cute I peeled them off and put them on my refrigerator."

"Did anyone else have eyes on their mailbox?" he asked.

She paused for a minute before answering, "I don't think so. I'm sure I would have noticed."

Faust ran downstairs to check. There were no other decorations on anyone's mailbox. Others would pick up their mail after her. He didn't like this.

Taking two stairs at a time, he checked outside her door to

make sure it wasn't marked in some way. Faust relaxed a bit not finding anything there.

As he reentered the apartment, Molly stood at the door with the two googly eye stickers on one finger. "You can leave those on your refrigerator if you wish, Little girl."

"You think there's something wrong?" she asked.

"Just keep your eyes open, Pixie. It bothers me when they mark the apartments of a single woman. Maybe you should come stay with me at the compound."

"Don't be silly. I can't just move in with you."

"Of course you can."

She stared at him. "We haven't even…"

"That's not a requirement."

"But everyone will assume," Molly pointed out.

"I'm okay with that."

"What?" Molly propped her hands on her hips and looked at him with an expression Faust could only describe as peeved.

"No one needs to know what goes on between the two of us," Faust told her. "They will have no idea that I'm stripping off your clothes in exactly thirty seconds and pinning you against that door to fill you with my cock."

He stroked a hand over his rapidly stiffening cock. He'd had a semi-hardon all day. Just the thought of Molly made him lose track of everything he was doing.

"You're going to what?"

"Take off your panties, Pixie."

"Here?" She stared at him. He loved the flush that started rising up from her modest dress's neckline.

"Now."

With an "eep!" she reached under her dress and tugged down her panties. Stepping out of them, she picked up the scrap of fabric and looked around as if wondering what to do with them.

Faust held his hand out. "Mine."

He watched her swallow hard and walk forward. She folded

them nicely before placing them in his hand. Faust lifted the material to his nose and inhaled deeply. Her eyes widened.

Lowering the lacey garment, he tucked it in his pocket. "Now the dress, Molly."

She tangled her fingers in the material and tugged it slightly upward, revealing her calves before freezing. "You want me to take it off?"

"Unless you want me to tear it off you, Little girl."

Molly shook her head and lifted the garment a bit higher. "I'm not very good at this."

"You have been with the wrong guys, Molly. You're going to be very good at riding my cock."

"I've only done it once. He wasn't very impressed," she whispered.

"Then he's a dumb fuck and a loser as a lover."

Faust walked forward and pulled her dress over her head, tossing it away. He stroked over her body loving every dip, curve, and straight line of her body. How could anyone make love to this sweet woman and walk away? That thought rocked him. He'd never gone into a relationship looking for something long-term. Now, he knew he'd never accept anything else.

"Molly. Look at me."

Her gaze focused on his and he could tell she expected something entirely different to come out of his mouth. Her shoulders sagged inward as if she were hiding herself from him.

"You're mine, Little girl. After this, I'm never letting you go."

Surprise spread over her face and the corners of her mouth tilted up before she visibly forced herself to guard against being hurt. "Maybe you should have sex with me before shackling yourself to me for a long time."

"I should wash your mouth out with soap for being so negative about yourself. Who knows, maybe I'm a horrible lover and you'll want to get away from me?"

Her spontaneous giggles broke the growing tension. Thank goodness.

"I'll take that as a compliment, Little girl. I think I promised sex against that door."

He watched her gaze dart past him to look at the wooden barrier. Faust reached over his head and dragged off his T-shirt. Tossing it away, he unfastened his jeans, providing room for his burgeoning cock. After pressing a kiss to the side of her neck, he smoothed over her shoulders and eased the straps of her bra down her arms. Faust leaned down to kiss her, loving the way she rose onto her tiptoes to meet his lips.

Passion flared between them as their tongues tangled and teased each other. Faust ripped his mouth from hers to taste her skin, leaving a trail of kisses down her neck and over one shoulder. Unfastening her sensible bra, he eased it off. He stroked his thumbs over the sides of her small breasts as he looked over her body.

"Damn, Pixie."

"Your muscles have muscles," she blurted, tracing her fingers over his chest and abdomen. When she dared follow the line of hair disappearing into the waistband of his boxer briefs, she froze when her fingers brushed something else.

"It can't be that long," she told him, leaning back to check him out.

"You are going to kill me, Pixie." Faust knew the minute he freed his shaft he'd fight himself to stay out of her. "Talk first. I've been tested and I'll wear a condom. Are you on birth control?"

She shook her head. "I did go get tested at one of those free clinics and I was okay."

"We'll go to a doctor together to get birth control for you tomorrow."

"You don't have to go with me," she blurted and turned a delightful shade of pink.

"I care about your health, Pixie. We'll go together. I won't go back in the exam room with you unless you decide you want me there."

"Okay," she whispered.

"Now, I think I promised you sex."

"Against the door," she reminded him helpfully.

He scooped her up in his arms and stalked toward the door. Molly wrapped her arms and legs around him, pressing her core against his shaft. Tantalized by her wiggles, Faust held her in place with one arm under her bottom. He kissed her deeply and loved her enthusiastic response. Molly might be new to love-making, but she was eager and responsive. He could feel her heat against his shaft.

Focused on her pleasure, Faust captured one pink nipple in his mouth. He lashed his tongue across it before drawing it into his mouth. Easing the suction when she dug her fingernails into his shoulders, Faust loved that she was so sensitive.

Lavishing the same treatment on her other breast, Faust rubbed himself against her pussy. His briefs became wet as they moved together. He mentally reminded himself to go slow. Faust inserted a hand between their bodies to explore. Her juices coated his fingertips as he stroked them through her pussy. Teasing her opening, Faust pressed a finger into her and groaned as she squeezed her muscles tight.

His cock jerked in his now too tight briefs as he imagined what it would feel like inside her. He needed to be in her now. Gritting his teeth, he pressed another finger inside her tight channel and scissored his fingers to stretch her. Molly tightened her hands on his shoulders and pressed kissed to his neck and shoulders.

"Please," she begged.

Unable to deny her, Faust grabbed a condom from his pocket and lifted the package to his mouth. Biting down on one edge to hold it, he freed up his hand. Faust thrust it into his briefs, roughly cupping his cock and balls to pull them from soaked material. It took all his willpower to not dive inside her immediately as he felt her wetness wrap around him directly. Gritting his teeth, he supported her with one arm as he pushed his jeans and briefs over his hips. Seconds later, he rolled the condom over his shaft.

Fitting the head of his cock against her opening, Faust forced himself to enter her slowly. Heat surrounded his shaft, pushing his arousal into overdrive. He could feel her body easing around him as he glided deeper.

"Faust," she moaned.

"You feel amazing, Pixie," he told her before kissing her hard.

When he reached a point of resistance, Faust withdrew a bit before pushing forward again. She wiggled, trying to hurry him up. After kissing a spot on her shoulder, Faust bit down firmly and flexed his hips. Her gasp went straight to his cock as he sank fully inside her. He forced himself to wait, giving her time to recover.

To his delight, she urged, "Move. If you don't move, I'm going to…"

She didn't get that threat finished. Faust withdrew and thrust fully into her body, drawing a moan from their throats. He repeated that motion and rubbed the root of his cock against her clit. The door rattled behind her as he plunged into her over and over.

He could feel small quivers around his shaft and knew she was close to her orgasm. Faust leaned back slightly to order, "Touch yourself, Pixie. Make yourself come around my cock."

She looked at him in amazement as if she couldn't believe what he had asked her to do. When his gaze held hers without wavering, Molly stroked a hand over his chest and abdomen to the place they were connected. He closed his eyes at the delectable feel of her fingertips brushing over the base of his shaft to touch herself.

Within seconds, she exploded around him. That wet hand trailed up his chest to wrap around his shoulders. Molly clung to him as she rocked her pussy against him, extending her pleasure. She pressed hot kisses to his neck before capturing his mouth in a sizzling exchange.

When her body calmed, Molly admitted, "I've never... Well, only with my vibrator. Your turn now."

"Oh, no, Pixie. You'll come on my cock at least four more times before we come together."

She stared at him in shock. "Is that even possible?"

Faust didn't answer but rubbed himself hard against her before pulling out fully and driving back into her heat. She pressed herself against the door as she peeked between their bodies to watch him move in and out of her. Her gaze ricocheted to meet his.

"Mine, Pixie. Your pussy is mine now." He pushed his hips a bit closer, enjoying her gasp as he filled every bit of space inside her.

Her climax struck immediately, cementing his suspicion that she enjoyed dirty talk. His lips curved in a carnal smile. He would enjoy making her blush as she came on his cock.

"Can you hear the door banging, Little one?"

"I hear it."

"So can your neighbors."

Her gasp made him speed up his thrusts.

"They're going to know I've fucked you deep and hard."

"Faust!" she whispered—her expression horrified and so turned on.

"And that you enjoyed every minute of it," he growled into her ear.

Her fingers tightened on his shoulders. Faust had already figured out that was her first tell. Changing his angle slightly, he cupped one small breast and tweaked her nipple between his thumb and finger.

Molly threw a hand over her mouth as she screamed. Her climax shook her body and Faust struggled to maintain his control. To distract himself, Faust whispered, "You're never going to look at this door without feeling me this deep inside you, Molly."

"Never," she mumbled through her hand as she bounced on his shaft.

"When you're in my space, no muffling your sweet sounds, Molly. Everyone at the clubhouse will know that your Daddy takes good care of you. Don't worry, your screams of pleasure will mix with the other Littles'."

Her eyes widened. Faust allowed her to imagine that image before shifting the arm that supported her to allow him to scoop up a bit of her slick juices and glide a finger to that hidden entrance between her buns. He tapped the tight ring of muscles, feeling it contract. Instantly, her body clamped around his shaft at the arousing, forbidden touch.

"No," she whispered.

"Yes," he corrected her. "Daddy's in charge. I'll take you everywhere, Little girl."

Her breathing quickened again. "Daddy…"

"And you know what?"

"What?" she whispered.

"You're going to love feeling my cock glide in and out of your bottom, stretching you and stroking past all these nerve endings." He pushed the tip of his finger into her tight opening. That was all she needed.

"Daddy!" she yelled, beyond caring about her neighbors.

This time, Faust allowed himself to come, emptying himself into the condom within her. She dropped her cheek onto his shoulder as she relaxed completely against him. Her trust that he would support and take care of her unlocked something inside him. She was his forever.

CHAPTER
TEN

Molly felt her face heat the next morning as she left for work. She'd already lost several minutes recreating last night in flashes each time she passed the wooden door. Faust was right. She'd never look at that door again without feeling him inside her. Simply touching it boosted the memories even more. Swallowing hard to control her desire, she walked through the door and locked it. Molly tried to act normal as she walked down the stairs and to her car. Thank goodness for the cool morning air!

There was something under her windshield wiper. Molly stopped and plucked the sucker out. It was blue and looked homemade. She knew Faust hadn't made lollipops, but she didn't doubt that Bear or Gabriel would make them for the Littles. Faust must have left one for her.

Not willing to lose the minty clean feeling of her freshly brushed teeth, Molly decided to save the treat for later. She tucked it in her purse and slid into the driver's seat. There wasn't a lot of traffic in her apartment complex at that time, so she was surprised when a car appeared behind her.

Alerted by something that made her keep track of him, Molly noticed he turned where she did. On a whim, she stopped and ran through a drive-thru for fancy coffee. When she came out of the shop's parking lot, the same car pulled in behind her.

Molly drove slowly to the church, willing the man to join the cars whipping around her. He didn't. When she turned into the church's driveway, the car hesitated then continued straight.

Heaving a sigh of relief, Molly grabbed her things and dashed into the church. She instantly felt protected. Who would invade a church to do bad things?

The two ministers were already in their offices when she walked in. Lester hollered for coffee while Steve called "Good morning."

"Good morning, gentlemen. I'll get coffee on right now," she promised.

As the coffee brewed, she checked the messages on the phone. Several she could take care of herself. Others required personal attention by the ministers. Molly grabbed a cup of coffee for each man and delivered them.

"I'm noting your late arrivals on my calendar," Lester informed her before taking a sip of the hot beverage she'd just handed him. He picked up a red marker and drew a large star on the day's date on his desk calendar.

"Actually my work day is supposed to start at nine. It's eight forty-five now. I arrived almost thirty minutes before I was supposed to be here," Molly answered, forcing herself to be assertive.

"Arguing with your boss is not a good idea, Molly."

She watched him draw an X over the star with a black pen. "I'm not arguing, Lester. I'm simply pointing out that I'm still early for my job requirements."

"I'm going to consider this level two of arguing." He circled the symbol on his calendar. "Don't reach the third."

Clamping her lips shut, Molly walked back to her desk. She was almost shaking with the combined tension of being followed to work and Lester's management style. That would be the last cup of coffee she poured him.

Glancing at the time, she saw she had ten minutes before she officially had to be at her desk working. Quickly, she pulled up her contract she'd filed on her phone electronically and printed it off. She tucked a dollar in the copy machine jar to pay for the paper when anyone made a personal copy. Returning to her desk, she placed it in a file to have ready.

No one would do this to Faust. She was too nice. Jerks like Lester enjoyed trampling all over people like her. No more.

Her temper cooled down as she worked. Molly enjoyed her job. She felt like her role was important and the congregation members were always pleasant to her.

At lunch time, she decided to go outside for lunch. She only had a few crackers left. Molly shook her head. She'd been so busy with Faust she lost track of things. Tonight, she had to stop at the store to get some things that would be easy to bring for lunch.

Munching on a cracker, she checked her phone. There were two messages from Faust.

Good morning, Little girl. I missed holding you while you slept.

Would you like to take a ride on my bike tonight?

While the first made her smile, the second was a bit nerve-racking. She thought for another minute before answering.

Hi, Faust. I'm afraid I need to stop at the store to pick up some things for lunch. I've destroyed this box of crackers.

A minute later her phone buzzed.

Daddy. Tell me you're eating something more nutritious than crackers.

I like crackers.

We'll go to the store after dinner.

Molly looked at the phone and shrugged. If he wanted to go to the store with her, okay. She ate the last few crackers in the box and stood up from the picnic table set up for people to enjoy. Taking a couple last deep breaths, she headed back to her desk.

The box rattled as she dropped it in the trashcan in the office.

"Molly. Coffee," Lester's voice called.

She hesitated and then deliberately sat down at her desk. If he was going to be mean, she wasn't going to wait on him. Diving back into her tasks for the day, Molly ignored his second call.

"Molly. Are you deaf?" Lester demanded, standing next to her desk.

"No, Lester. Simply busy."

"Not too busy to lounge outside," he said with a snort.

"It was lovely outside. I enjoyed my lunch break," she answered with a smile even though she was steaming inside.

"It must be nice to just quit working."

"The coffee tank is full," she said, ignoring his implication that she wasn't doing enough.

"You really shouldn't be so lazy. It doesn't look good on your evaluations."

"What's this about evaluations?" Steve asked, walking back into the office.

"We're discussing how actions are reflected in evaluations," Lester answered in an easy-going tone that was markedly different than how he'd talked to Molly earlier.

"Lester is concerned that I arrived late the last two mornings, took my lunch break outside, and was too lazy to get him coffee when he bellowed from his office," Molly told her boss.

"You were here well before nine when the office opens. Heavens knows if we added up all the time you give us for free before and after our office hours, you could probably take vacation for several weeks," Steve said before looking at Lester. "Molly is busy. She's kind to bring us coffee. It's not her job to wait on us. And lunch outside sounds like an amazing break. I don't see anything wrong with that. Perhaps, Lester, you should bring any concerns you have to me rather than discussing them with Molly. You are not her direct supervisor."

"Just making sure the church is getting what it's paying for," Lester answered lightly.

"Speaking of pay, Molly, we need to discuss your salary.

Schedule a time for the two of us to talk tomorrow," Steve requested.

"I'd like to sit in on that meeting," Lester requested.

"That's not necessary. Did you get the volunteers for the chili competition?" Steve asked him.

"I did. Great people."

"Who did you talk to?" Steve asked.

"Oh, I don't remember names now. I'd have to look at the list," Lester said quickly.

"Let's go over that now," Steve requested and gestured for Lester to precede him down the hall.

Molly worked hard to control her facial expression. Lester didn't remember who was on the list because she'd gotten the volunteers. She tried not to listen in on their conversation in the head minister's office, but it was obvious that Steve knew Lester had pawned the job off on her instead of taking care of it.

Feeling like she needed to celebrate, Molly remembered the lollipop in her purse. That would be the perfect sweet treat. She pulled it out of the wrapper just as the phone rang in the office. Startled, Molly bobbled the sucker and dropped it on the floor as she scrambled to answer the phone. When she picked it up a few minutes later, she wrinkled her nose at the dirt already clinging to the sugary treat and dropped it in the trash.

CHAPTER
ELEVEN

Thank goodness the rest of the day went well. Molly hadn't even seen Lester after his talk with Steve. She didn't understand why some people saw their position as one of power while others saw theirs as a place of service. It was such a different viewpoint.

Before pushing the door open, she scanned the parking lot. Instead of seeing that car from the morning commute, she spotted Faust relaxed on his bike. Popping through the door, she practically skipped across the parking lot to greet him.

"Hi!" she said, feeling shy after all their passion from the previous night.

"No kiss in the church parking lot?"

"Can I give you two later?" she asked, looking around.

"Five and you have a deal."

She couldn't help grinning at him. "Deal."

"We need to go grab some groceries for you," he stated.

"I do. You don't have to go with me."

"We're both off work. We want to spend time together. While I'd rather be buried balls deep inside your sweet body instead of in the store, it's important you have something to eat other than crackers for lunch."

"Faust!" she protested, looking around.

"No one can hear me, Little girl. Do you know someone who drives a dark sedan?" Faust asked, reciting the license plate from memory.

"That sounds like the car that kept following me this morning."

The look on his face scared her. "There was someone following you and you didn't call me?"

"No, silly. You were at work. I tried a few things like running through a drive-thru for coffee and making a few strange turns. He drove past when I pulled into the church parking lot."

"Whether I'm a work or not, you call me if anything like this ever happens again. Immediately."

He held her gaze captive until she agreed. "You know you're not responsible for me."

"What do you think being your Daddy means?"

"Faust. Shhh!" she urged, looking around to make sure the parking lot was empty. Her eyes landed on something blue on her windshield. "Oh, you left me another sucker."

"We're not finished with this discussion, Pixie, and what sucker?"

"There was a lollipop under my windshield wiper this morning. I thought you'd left it there."

"Did you eat it?" he demanded, swinging his leg over his bike.

"No." She shook her head frantically. "What's wrong? You didn't leave it?"

"I'll never leave anything where people could mess with it, Molly. That's not safe."

She trailed after Faust as he walked the short distance to her car. He grabbed the candy with his gloved fingers, holding it carefully as he looked it over. "You don't think it's just a lollipop, do you?"

"No, Pixie. I don't. I'll get this to a friend of the club to see what it is. Let's go to your house to get your stuff."

"I was going to stop and pick up something for lunches," she reminded him.

"The clubhouse has lots of stuff you can take each day. If you don't mind leftovers, Gabriel will put a meal in a container for you to microwave or I'll make you a sandwich."

"That's way out of my way to stop each morning at the clubhouse," she pointed out.

"It won't be when you're rolling out of my bed each day."

"You want me to move in with you?"

"There's no want about this. You are moving in with me. Someone's targeting you. They know where you live and work. No one's going to mess with you or your car on Shadowridge Guardian territory."

"That's frightening, Faust," she said, trying to keep from panicking.

"It's scaring the crap out of me, too."

That made her swallow hard. "You're not afraid of anything."

"I'm afraid of someone hurting you."

"Okay. I'll come stay with you," she whispered.

"Your leather-wearing, tattooed boyfriend is going to scare people away, Molly. You should consider who you hang out with. It reflects on you."

Faust calmly put the candy in his pocket before turning to face the assistant minister who stood by his own car a couple spaces away. "I thought churches welcomed anyone to attend."

"Don't challenge him, Faust. Nothing I do is going to be right in his eyes," Molly urged, wrapping her hands around his arm to hold him back.

"I'll call the police on both of you if you threaten me," Lester threw out as he jumped in his car.

They heard the click of the locks before he reversed out of the space and squealed his tires to get away.

"That guy needs to be careful with his tires. If he gets a flat, who's going to help him?" Faust commented dryly.

"He's a jerk."

"And a minister?"

"He's done all the study. He just missed the point of a few passages in the bible," Molly suggested. "Come on. Let's go get my stuff."

"I have an appointment for you first at a clinic I trust. Follow me over there and honk if you see that car. I want to talk to him."

"Now? I'm not ready, Faust." Her mind raced with the embarrassment of one of those exams. She hadn't shaved her legs this morning and they'd just made love last night. Would the doctor be able to tell?

"You're fine, Pixie. I'll be there with you."

"Really, can't we go another night? There's so much to do tonight."

"No, Little girl. You'll just worry, and it will get harder another time. Follow me."

He held her gaze until she dropped her head down slightly. "I'm worrying now."

"I'll be there with you, Pixie. I promise it will be okay."

"You're kinda bossy," she accused.

"Exactly. Let's go. In the car. Follow me."

"Yes, Sir!"

"Daddy."

"Faust!" Molly looked around again to make sure they were still alone. Relaxing a bit when she saw the coast was clear, she unlocked her car to allow him to help her inside.

In a few minutes, they were off. Molly was sure Faust had to feel like a grandma driving slow enough for her to follow him. She was the exact opposite of a dare devil behind the wheel. To her surprise, they didn't pull into a seedy clinic but into the parking lot of a sleek, modern facility. She parked and jumped out of the car.

"I don't know if my insurance will cover me here, Faust. I can go back to the free clinic I went to before," Molly told him.

"Let's get your purse and close your door. Trust me, Little one."

Molly looked back to see her door standing wide open and her keys still in the ignition. "I'm an idiot." She rushed back to follow his instructions.

When she had it all together, Faust took her hand and led her into the building. He gave their names at the reception desk and guided her to two empty seats in the corner when they were checked in and given forms to fill out.

"Do you need help with the forms, Pixie?"

"I can do it." Trying to block out the feel of Faust next to her, she filled in the first bits of information. When she got to the more private questions, she peeked over at Faust. He was looking at something on his phone. She leaned a bit closer to see he was reading what looked like a novel.

"Are you reading a book?" burst from her mouth.

"Are you assuming I don't know how to read?" Faust asked with one raised eyebrow.

"Oh, I didn't mean anything bad like that. I just expected you to be watching..." Molly leaned forward and whispered, "Porn."

"I don't need to watch porn now. I have you," he said in a normal voice.

An older woman got up and moved to the other side of the waiting room. "Look. You made her move," Molly hissed, waving a hand in the woman's direction.

"She got up all by herself, Pixie. Do you need help with those questions?" Faust asked.

"No. I've got this."

Turning back to the forms, Molly watched out of the corner of her eye to see Faust return to reading. Quickly filling them in, she took the clipboard to the receptionist. As she handed it over, Molly asked, "I don't know if you take my insurance."

"We take almost everything. Let me make copies of your insurance card and your ID."

In a minute, the receptionist handed them back with a brochure. "Here's all the services we provide. If you don't have a doctor you prefer to see, Dr. Rhodes is taking new patients."

"Oh, I don't have a doctor. My insurance doesn't pay for much, so I don't go. This was important."

"Talk to the doctor. Basic care like a physical, preventative inoculations, etc. are covered here at no cost."

"Thanks."

Molly didn't believe that. The insurance the church provided for the ministers, herself, and the janitor was the barest minimum. She was just glad she had some.

When she sat down, Molly stowed all her cards away and sat quietly. She didn't pull out her own phone. She'd spent enough time on her computer during the day. Faust held his hand out and she linked her fingers with his. He squeezed her hand.

"You're okay," he told her quietly.

"What is this place? It looks brand new. Much different than the clinic I went to. You don't have to come back with me," she blurted at the end of her stream of thought.

"I'll come back with you and will leave any time you want me to."

"They're going to weigh me in and do all the doctor stuff."

"You've been in my arms, Little girl. I know how much you weigh. Numbers on a scale don't mean anything to me. Nor does your weight."

She looked at him in astonishment. Molly hadn't considered he already knew what she weighed. One glance at his biceps told her she could eat all the dessert she wanted, and he wouldn't have any problems. Letting out a small sigh of relief, Molly let go of all the things rumbling around in her head.

"Hey. Let's try this game."

Faust levered his phone in front of him so she could see the display. It counted down from five to one before displaying a word.

"What do I do?" she asked.

"Say other things to get me to guess that word," Faust explained. "We want to get as many words guessed right as we can."

"Really? Okay. Black. Legs. Hairy. Web."

"Spider."

"A kind of one of those," she said, leaning forward a bit.

"Tarantula," Faust guessed.

"Yes!"

He tilted his phone toward her and then back straight. Tarantula disappeared and another word appeared. Molly blurted the word out and then blinked up at him.

"Did you say the word?" he asked with a hint of a smile that erased some of his usual fierce expression.

"Sorry!"

"No problem. Try again."

This time she contained her urge to say the word aloud and started to describe it. This time, it only took Faust two words to figure out the right answer. This was fun.

By the time the nurse called her name, Molly had stopped fretting about where she was. She was having fun with Faust.

"That's you, Pixie," Faust told her gently as he stood up.

"Oh. Sorry!"

Molly walked to the door and stammered, "Is it okay if Faust comes back with me?"

"Of course," the nurse said without any hesitation.

In a few minutes, she was in an exam room and was amazed that her blood pressure had been in the normal range. Usually, she was too nervous when she went to the doctor. When the nurse left, she didn't even ask Molly to take all her clothes off.

"Hi, Molly. I'm Dr. Rhodes. It's nice to meet you."

"Hi, Dr. Rhodes. This is my..." she paused, unsure how to introduce Faust.

"I'm Faust, Molly's partner," Faust volunteered.

That sounds permanent.

"Molly, are you okay with Faust being in the exam room with you and hearing our conversation?" Dr. Rhodes asked.

"Yes. That's fine. I'd tell him everything anyway."

"Okay. So, I see you don't have a regular doctor and you're here for birth control?"

"Yes, please. Do I have to get undressed?" Molly said apprehensively.

"Probably not. Let me ask you a few questions to see how healthy you are and if you fit any risk categories for birth control that would entail a more invasive exam."

Molly nodded. She liked how the doctor listened to her answers and did an efficient exam to listen to her heart and lungs. She felt like Dr. Rhodes cared while being skilled and practical.

"You're young and in good health. You don't have any conditions that would make me hesitate to prescribe birth control pills —no smoking, diabetes, stroke, cancer, etc. I think we can start you on a prescription today."

Dr. Rhodes paused and looked at each of them. "Birth control won't protect you from communicable diseases. You've both been tested after your last partners?"

"Yes," Molly told her.

"Yes, Doctor," Faust confirmed.

"I like that you're here together. I don't see that often. Molly, here's your prescription and a pamphlet on birth control. Read it carefully so you take it correctly and use a second form of birth control until you've taken an entire pack of pills to be fully protected. You do need a physical including a pelvic exam if you are sexually active. I am accepting new patients if you'd like to make an appointment with me."

"Thank you, Dr. Rhodes."

"She'll do that, Doctor."

"Molly, I think you've got a good one here. Let me walk you up to the front to check out."

When they reached the parking lot, Faust pulled her into his arms and hugged her. "Let's go get pizza. We can drop your prescription off at the pharmacist first and it will be ready when we finish eating."

"Faust, I need to wait until I get paid. I'll have to budget for this."

"Not happening, Little girl. It benefits us both. I'll pay."

"But it's my medicine."

"Only because they don't have birth control pills for men. When they do, you can buy them for me," he suggested. "For now, you can go with me to get pizza."

"I am hungry," she confessed. "Am I really moving in with you tonight? Are the Guardians going to be okay with some random woman moving in?"

"You're mine, Pixie. There's nothing random about it."

CHAPTER
TWELVE

"Hi, Molly. I'm glad to see you back," Gabriel called from the kitchen when they walked in.

"Hi, Gabriel."

"Have you eaten?"

"Yes, thank you. We had pizza," Molly explained. She looked up at him repeatedly. He knew she was wondering why the man greeted her and not Faust.

Pressing an arm to her lower back, Faust urged her closer to the kitchen island where Gabriel stood as he pulled her suitcase behind him. "Hey, got anything for a Little girl's lunch tomorrow?"

"Leftover lasagna or crackers and cheese?" Gabriel asked.

"Lasagna, please, if it's not too much work. I've been eating crackers at work for a few days," Molly admitted.

"Gotcha. Lunches are absolutely no problem. If you'll tell me what you like and what you can't eat, I'll order somethings especially for you."

"Oh, I don't want to be a problem. I'll eat anything."

"Tell him what you told me at the restaurant," Faust urged.

"I can just pick them off. It's not a bother," Molly said quickly.

"She doesn't like mushrooms or bell peppers," Faust revealed for her.

"No allergies, Molly? Peanuts? Gluten?" Gabriel asked, pulling out his phone to make some notes.

"No. I'm not allergic to anything. I can pick out mushrooms and peppers."

"Not happening. Everyone has their favorites and yuck foods. I'll make sure your meals are free from the things you don't like. What kind of pizza did you have?" Gabriel asked.

"My favorite, pepperoni!" she shared.

"And what do you know—that's Faust's favorite, too," Gabriel mentioned.

"I know. That's fun."

"Molly, I should be up in the morning when you leave but if not, I'm going to leave your lunch in refrigerator two. I'll label a place with your name." Gabriel opened the fridge to show her several of the Littles' names hanging down. There were colorful lunch bags with their names written on them.

"Are you sure it's not an imposition?" Molly asked.

"Not at all. I'm glad to know you're getting something good for lunch," Gabriel assured her as he closed the door and walked back to the counter.

"Could you have someone check this out?" Faust asked, pulling the lollipop he'd found tucked under Molly's windshield wiper. "She's had a couple left on her car."

"I don't like that," Gabriel said. His expression hardened to rival Faust's.

"Daddy, I… Never mind, I can see you're busy," Eden said, turning around.

"Back here, Little girl," Gabriel ordered. "What have you done wrong?"

"Nothing? You just looked so pissed off, I thought I should give you time to relax," Eden said quickly.

"You weren't the one who shook up my favorite beer at the bar?" he asked.

Eden shook her head quickly.

"There are cameras in the common's room, Ladybug."

Eden looked at Faust to confirm that fact. When he nodded solemnly, Eden quickly apologized. "I shouldn't have. It slipped and then I thought maybe it would be funny. They say beer is good to condition your hair. I bet your beard will gleam."

"Go tell that to Storm. He's the one that got sprayed," Gabriel suggested, pointing at the muscular man whose T-shirt was plastered to his skin.

"Storm?" Eden swallowed hard.

"Let's go congratulate him on his glistening beard," Gabriel suggested, circling the island to take her hand.

"He won't spank me, will he?" Eden's words drifted to them as they moved away.

"He won't," Gabriel assured her.

"She's in so much trouble, isn't she?" Molly whispered.

"Definitely," Faust assured her. "But Storm will understand."

"Does he have a Little girl?"

"Not yet."

"That's sad." Molly watched Eden confess that she had shaken up the beer to get her Daddy. Storm accepted her apology with a very stern look and warned her not to do that again.

"Let's get you settled in my apartment, Pixie," Faust said, guiding her to a doorway.

"Are you sure it's okay for me to be here?"

"Yes." He opened the door and ushered her inside. "It's not very exciting in here. I don't spend a lot of time in my apartment."

The guys did all gather in the clubhouse section. There was so much going on there. Even in a crowd, Faust seemed alone. It surprised her that Faust chose to be with the others instead of alone.

"What's going on in your head, Pixie? Do we need to change something in here to make you comfortable?"

"Oh, no. You don't need to change anything for me," she told him quickly. "You don't seem to like people a lot."

"And you're wondering why I'm not a hermit in my room?"

"I don't mean to offend you," she rushed to say.

"No offense, Little girl. You're right. I don't care about most people. Just those that matter."

Molly smiled at him. She felt that simple statement inside her. She mattered to Faust. That meant a lot.

She darted forward to wrap her arms around his waist and squeeze him tight. "You're important to me, too, Faust."

"Daddy."

"He's important to me, too," Molly quipped.

"It's past your bedtime, Little girl. Let's get you unpacked. Then it's time for a bath then bed."

"It's eight o'clock, F… Daddy," she corrected herself.

"You've had a long day. Do you not wish to take a bath?"

"Do you have bubbles?" she joked.

"Definitely."

Her jaw dropped as she stared at him. "No way. You don't take bubble baths."

"That's very judgmental of you, Pixie. Let's get your night clothes."

Unpacking that statement, Molly watched Faust lift her suitcase onto the bed. He unzipped and opened it.

"You might as well leave it in there. I'll just put it over there in the corner," Molly told him, moving to lift it.

"Stop right there, Little girl."

Molly froze at his order. She watched him disappear into the closet and come back with empty hangers.

"You get started on hanging up the clothes that should go in the closet." She picked up a dress as she watched him open a drawer. He pulled out a couple of folded T-shirts, leaving it empty.

"You can put your undies in here. The drawer below is empty."

"You don't have very many things in there," she said in surprise.

"How many pairs of jeans and T-shirts does a man need?"

She shrugged, not knowing the answer. Molly told him, "Thank you."

"Of course, Pixie."

Molly gasped as he scooped her practical cotton panties and bras out of the corner of the suitcase and put them in the dresser.

"I've touched your pussy, Pixie. I think I'm allowed to touch your underwear," Faust reminded her.

She watched the corners of his mouth curve upward. Giggles burst from her mouth as her tension evaporated. When he joined her laugher with a deep chuckle of amusement, Molly loved it.

I love him.

Trying to hide her shock at that realization, Molly busied herself with emptying the suitcase. Faust didn't ask her any questions, but she caught him watching her. She thought about telling him but didn't know how to do it. What if he didn't feel the same about her?

When the suitcase was empty, Molly allowed Faust to guide her into the bathroom. Seeing a cup with a solitary toothbrush, she realized she'd forgotten hers.

"Oh, no. I didn't bring my toothbrush," Molly lamented. She'd have to grab one on the way home.

"I've got you, Pixie." She watched him open the bottom drawer. Inside was a jumble of toothbrushes.

"What's your favorite color?"

"Purple."

"You're in luck. I have one here," he said, plucking up a package.

"Did you rob a dentist?" she asked, looking at all the tooth-pastes, mouthwash mini bottles, and floss. So many different types of floss.

"My dad's a dentist. He sends me a box of supplies every so often. Help yourself to anything you like."

"Thank you. I can't stand not to have clean teeth," she confessed.

"You can thank my dad someday when we visit my folks. I'm going to raid the Little supply closet for bubble bath and whatever else catches my eye. Potty. I'll be back to help you in the bathtub."

"Can I go?" she blurted.

When he raised one eyebrow in a silent question, Molly said, "I've never seen supplies for Littles. What's in there?"

Faust looked at his watch and then back at her. "Five minutes when we get there. We can go back and explore later if you don't have enough time."

"Okay!" she said, trying not to bounce up and down.

Shaking his head, Faust walked over and started the bathtub. He adjusted the temperature before holding out his hand to her. "Let's go. It's right across the hall."

She dashed to his side and squeezed his hand. Together, they negotiated their way out the doorways and into the hall. There, Molly took several quick steps to keep up with Faust's long strides as they turned the corner.

"You have long legs, Daddy."

"I do. It's right here."

When he opened the closet door at the end of the hall and switched on the light, Molly crowded in front of him. As she tried to take in all the different items included in the supply cabinet, Molly knew her eyes had widened to their absolute limit. Pacifiers. Sippy glasses. Oh, shit—a set of anal plugs.

"Do you want bubblegum, strawberry, or lavender bubble bath?" Faust asked.

"Wow. Lavender," she chose, amazed she had a choice.

"What else would you like, Pixie?"

"Oh, I don't need anything."

"Let's get you a cup. Want kitties, flowers, or kisses?" he asked.

"Kisses."

Faust dropped a kiss on the top of her head and reached over her again to scoop up a pink cup with lipstick prints all over it. Molly tried not to look at a pacifier on the second shelf. She'd always wanted to try one. That one was pretty. It was purple with a pink ring.

"Thank you, Daddy," she said, stepping back to leave.

"I think we need a few more things." He picked up a set of bath toys featuring mermaids and floating shells, a Little girl alert doorhanger, a fancy hair clip, and his hand hovered over the purple and pink pacifier. "Will you try one of these for your Daddy?"

She nodded so hard she thought her head might pop off.

"Good girl. Ready for your bath?"

"Let's go!" she encouraged, remembering the water gushing into the tub.

"Hang this on the door for Daddy. I have my hands full," Faust requested, wiggling the Little girl alert sign. As she hooked it on the doorknob, Molly noticed several doors already had them.

"We'll write your name on the dotted line tomorrow," he told her.

She grinned at him as he opened the door and ushered her inside. The bathtub was about half full when they reached it. Faust set the items they had gathered on the vanity before moving to the side of the tub. After testing the temperature with his hand, Faust proclaimed it almost perfect and adjusted the water a bit before pouring in some bubble bath.

Immediately, the floral scent filled the room. Molly inhaled deeply and couldn't wait to get in the tub. Figuring she needed to do something, Molly stepped out of her shoes and picked them up, wondering what to do with them.

"My job," Faust said, taking them from her hand and setting them aside in the corner of the room. He gathered the bottom of her dress in his hands and lifted it over her head. He was so efficient in stripping off her bra and panties she didn't have time to protest.

"Go potty," he instructed before opening the small linen closet to pull out a couple big thirsty towels and a washcloth.

She waited for him to step outside so she could use the toilet, but he simply set the towels on the edge of the tub. When he leaned over to turn off the water, she knew that was her last chance to pee before he stood to watch her. Quickly, she took care of her business and returned to his side, embarrassed.

Faust helped her into the tub and got her settled before grabbing the bath set from the vanity. As she scooped the suds close to cover her body self-consciously, he opened the box and plopped the shells onto the top of the bubbles. When they disappeared, he suggested, "Maybe these are for non-sudsy baths? Should we save these for another day?"

"No, Daddy. The mermaids want to play," she assured him.

"Here, Pixie." He handed her the three mermaids.

After taking care of the box, Faust knelt by the tub and picked up the washcloth. He dipped it into the water before standing back up and grabbing the hair clip from the counter. She closed her eyes in delight as he smoothed her hair back away from her face. In seconds, he had it twisted and secured on top of her head.

"Close your eyes and I'll wash your face first."

She tried not to let herself wonder how he'd gotten so good at doing hair. Her expression must have given her away as he settled back on his knees.

Following his directions, she squeezed her eyes closed and sighed inwardly as he gently stroked the wet fabric over her features. "I have a younger sister who always wore her hair in pigtails. She was also a crazy kid on the playground. If you totaled it up, I'm sure I spent hours putting the scrunchies back in her hair."

"Oh. That's fun."

"It's a miracle I didn't end up as a hair stylist," he said.

Unable to resist the temptation, Molly peeked at him. Was he kidding?

He wagged his bushy eyebrows at her, and she burst into giggles. "Daddy! I can't imagine you dyeing hair and waxing eyebrows."

Again, he chuckled with her. She liked this side of Faust and knew he didn't share it with very many people. That idea made her feel warm inside.

"Play, Pixie. Can you find the shells?"

While she searched through the suds for a floating shell, he stroked the washcloth down her back. It felt so good. She arched her back silently asking him to continue.

"Pixie, I'm glad you're here. Whether I'm concerned about your safety or not, I like having you close. Think about staying here with your Daddy."

"Permanently?" she asked, turning her head to look at him.

"Yes, Little girl. I don't ever want to lose you."

"I have a morals clause in my contract. They could fire me any time," she shared, quietly.

"That would be a very bad move on their part," he said in a voice instantly dark with anger.

"It's a church. I understood it when I signed it. Forget I brought it up. If I have to choose between you and my job... I have to work to survive, Faust."

He finished her back and shifted in front of her slightly. "Mermaids in your right hand. How about if we worry about what might happen when it does? I'm here for you, Pixie. I won't flake out."

A snort of laughter burst from her. When Faust paused as he

washed her left arm and looked at her in concern, she said, "That was funny. You could never be a flake."

"No," he agreed as he washed all her fingers, massaging them.

That should not feel so good. She sighed with enjoyment as she dropped the mermaids to the bottom of the tub.

He swept the washcloth over her wrist and up her arm. On the downward stroke, his fingers brushed the side of her sensitive breast. Molly bit her bottom lip to keep a moan from escaping.

"No biting," he told her. "Let Daddy hear your sweet sounds. Right arm, now."

She extended it across her body eagerly and Faust repeated his soothing finger massage before washing her arm. Molly held her breath waiting to see where he would clean next. The air flooded back into her lungs as he stroked the soft terrycloth over her collar bones. Why did it feel so different when he washed her?

Faust swirled the washcloth around her small breasts and down her torso. When he reached her mound, he didn't hesitate but swept the cloth between her lower lips. The feel of the material changed there as the nubby fabric stroked over her most sensitive parts. She could feel warmth gathering between her thighs that had nothing to do with his carefully chosen water temperature.

"Daddy?" she whispered.

"I'm glad you love your Daddy's touch," he answered before moving on to wash her legs down to her toes.

That felt good, too, but Molly was on edge. She wanted more. Maybe he'll come back to help me come?

"Up on your knees, Pixie."

Reluctantly, she rose partially from the water. She tried to keep her expression from revealing her disgruntled feeling that he'd left her hanging. Molly reminded herself he wasn't responsible for pleasuring her.

Faust cupped her jaw and brought her lips to his for a fiery kiss. "I'm not ignoring your needs, Little girl. I'm getting you ready for bed."

"But..."

"No butts other than this cute one." He rubbed the washcloth over her derriere and slid it between her buttocks to clean her thoroughly. Faust dropped the cloth into the water behind her.

"All clean," he announced as he stood.

Plucking her out of the water as if she weighed nothing, Faust stood her on the mat and rubbed her skin dry. He wrapped her securely in a towel. "What else do you need to do before you go to sleep?" he asked.

"I need to put some lotion on my face and go to the bathroom."

Faust picked up a bottle that he'd unpacked earlier from her suitcase. "Is this it?"

"Yes." She rushed forward to squeeze a small amount on her fingers and rubbed it gently on her face.

"Go potty."

"I can meet you in the bedroom. Or wherever you want me to sleep."

"You'll sleep in my arms, Little girl. Go potty." Faust turned to the tub and opened the drain to let the water out.

She dragged her feet over to the toilet and sat down reluctantly. It seemed so intimate to pee in front of him. "Do I get to watch you pee?" she blurted.

"If you want, Pixie. There are no secrets between a Daddy and his Little girl," Faust told her as he fished the toys out of the draining water.

After finishing, she washed her hands at the sink. Molly watched Faust move to stand next to her. "All done, Daddy. I'm ready for bed."

"Good girl."

Faust scooped her up in his arms and carried her to the bedroom. When he set her on the edge of the bed, Molly tried to squirm off, not wishing to get the bedclothes wet. He held her in place as he stripped the wet towel from her body.

"Arms up," he directed and dropped the tattered, soft T-shirt she'd worn for years over her head.

She fingered the material before whispering, "I'm sorry this isn't fancier."

"I'm not attracted to you because of what you wear on the outside, Molly. If this is comfortable, that's what's important. If you want something to play dress up in, we'll get you something fancy."

"I think lace is scratchy," she confessed before whispering, "I do need some underwear."

"No panties in bed."

"Is that like the Shadowridge Guardian's rule?" she joked.

"No. That's Daddy's rule."

"Oh."

"Lean back, Pixie."

Molly started to twist herself around to stretch out in bed. Faust's hands closed around her thighs, holding her in place with her lower legs dangling over the side of the mattress. She looked up at him in confusion.

"Lie back, Little girl," he repeated. This time, he lowered himself to kneel between her legs.

A glimmer of understanding sparked in her mind. He wasn't going to...

Faust drew her thighs wide apart and pulled her bottom to the edge of the bed, throwing her slightly off balance. She dropped back to lean on her elbows. Placing a kiss on her mound, Faust paused to inhale deeply.

"I can smell your arousal, Pixie. I bet you'd sleep better if I had a tasty bedtime snack," he suggested before gliding his tongue along the crease of her pussy. "Delicious."

Molly felt like all the air had been sucked out of the room as he explored her with his mouth. Her fingers tightened on the comforter. Afraid he'd stop, she tried not to move.

Faust lifted one of her legs over his shoulder, exposing her further to his view. "So pretty."

She shivered as he studied her. A small noise burst from her lips as he waited for something. He had to help her come.

"I'm sorry, Pixie. I bet you're waiting for this," he suggested, lowering his mouth once again to her.

Faust slid his tongue through her sensitive folds to find her clit. Circling it with the tip of his tongue before pulling it gently into his mouth, he tantalized her. The view of his expressions and the intimate explorations enthralled Molly. She didn't know what to do but quickly decided she could just enjoy his attentions.

Sensations gathered inside her. She was so close to coming. A scream erupted from her throat when he thrust three fingers into her. The welcome invasion stretched and filled the need inside her.

Not pausing, Faust pushed her through that first orgasm into a second. Shaking, Molly fell off her elbows to lie flat on the mattress as her body shuddered with pleasure. She had no idea she could feel this much.

Softening his touch, Faust allowed her to come down from the high of her climax. Limp from her body's response, Molly didn't want to move. When he lifted his mouth from her several minutes later, she didn't open her eyes. She felt him rise to his feet.

Molly peeked up at him as he lifted her into his arms and turned her to rest on the pillows, straight on the bed. After tucking Angel into her arms, he covered her with the soft comforter and tucked it under her chin. Faust leaned close and pressed a kiss to her lips. There was something so sensual about tasting herself on his lips.

"Sleep, Pixie."

Nodding, she allowed herself to tumble into dreams that all seemed to revolve around one tall, tattooed biker.

CHAPTER
THIRTEEN

Bouncing with happiness after her day that included a conversation with Minister Steve and a raise, Molly couldn't wait to tell Faust. Just thinking his name made her blush and remember how well he touched her. Daydreaming about how they'd spend their evening, Molly walked out into the parking lot.

She was almost to her car when a man asked, "Why aren't you eating your lollipops?"

Startled by how close he was to her without her noticing him, Molly snapped to attention. "You need to leave me alone." She turned to keep him in sight as she backed toward her car.

"If you'll taste your treat, this will be so much easier on you."

"I don't know what you're talking about. Just leave me alone," she tried to keep the tremor of fear out of her voice and failed miserably.

If I scream, will Minister Steve hear me inside?

"Don't do anything stupid. That won't work out well for you."

"I could say the same thing to you." She grabbed at anything to say.

Bumping into her car with her bottom, Molly hoped the automatic locks would work this time. She fumbled with the button and heard clicks. "Look, the minister is coming," she said, looking past his shoulder toward the church.

When he fell for it and looked, she scrambled into the car and pushed the lock button. No clicks. She tried one more time before leaning to the side to press the key into the ignition. Her door started to open.

Molly cringed to the side and finally pushed the key into the ignition. Twisting it as she stomped on the brake, she begged for it to start. Please! Please! Please!

A hand wrapped around her arm just as the engine caught. Throwing the lever into drive, Molly floored the gas pedal and felt his nails tear her skin as she drove through the flower beds lining the parking lot to get away. She drove over the church's lawn to reach the driveway and burst onto the road. Other drivers honked and gestured rudely as they swerved and braked to avoid hitting her.

She drove like a wild woman, focused only on getting to Faust. The rattling car door finally captured her attention, and she dragged it closed. Reaching the Shadowridge Guardians' shop drive, Molly started honking frantically. She ricocheted up the drive and screeched to a stop as Kade walked out to see what was happening.

Their eyes met through the windshield as her car rocked back and forth inches from his powerful body from the hasty stop. Every inch of her body shook. She watched Kade open his mouth and yell for Faust.

Her Daddy came at a full run toward Kade and then circled around him to reach her door. He tried the handle.

"Molly, you're safe. Turn the car off and open the door," Faust urged.

She could hear the hidden anger in his voice as he tried to talk gently to her. Molly shook her head. She couldn't do it. The adrenaline evaporated from her body, leaving her paralyzed.

"Pixie? What happened?" Faust asked, lowering himself to her level.

All she could do was shake her head. The pain from her arm roared into life and she pried her hand off the steering wheel to rub her fingers over her upper arm. When she pulled them back, her fingers were covered in blood. She looked up at Faust who let out a string of curses before yelling.

"Doc! She's bleeding. I don't know if it's a bullet wound or something else."

A scratching sound at the passenger window made her jump. The car rolled a few inches forward, causing everyone to jump back.

Molly shook her head as she pressed down fully on the brake. She looked at Faust, willing him to help her. "Daddy..."

"I'm here, Pixie. I need you to put the car in park. Remi needs her Daddy to be safe. Move your right hand and shift the car into park. You can do this, Molly."

His absolute conviction got to her. She looked down again at the fresh red blood and wiped it carefully on her chest. Moving slowly, she turned slightly to her right and fitted her hand on the control.

"You're doing so well, Little girl. Push the lever forward."

Taking a deep breath, Molly followed his directions and felt the car settle. She relaxed back against the seat.

"Good girl. Ink's going to open the passenger door for you. It's okay. You know him."

That scratch came at the window again. This time, she watched a familiar figure insert a thin device into her car from the top of the window. Molly looked back at Faust and whispered, "I'm so scared, Daddy."

"I know. You're going to be in my arms in ten seconds, baby."

The sound of her passenger window dropping made her panic and she automatically pressed the gas. The engine roared as a hand reached in to push the unlock button. Instantly, Faust was on his feet, and he ripped the door open to pull her out. He carried her into the closest service bay.

Men swarmed her car, and she couldn't care less what happened to it.

"You're okay, Pixie," Faust told her as he hugged her tight.

"Daddy..." she whispered, clinging desperately to him as tears streamed from her eyes.

"You're safe, Little girl. I need to see your arm to see how hurt you are. Can I set you down?"

"No!" she yelled, scaring even herself.

"You hold her. I'll check out her arm," Doc said softly to Faust.

"Hi, Molly. I'm going to take a look at your arm so your Daddy doesn't freak out. Will that be okay?" Doc asked, gently raising her fluttery sleeve.

"Nail gouges," he reported a few seconds later.

Faust let out a string of curses that made Molly hide her face against his neck.

"Get it under control, Faust. You can get mad later," Doc reminded him.

"I'm in control. If not, someone would already be dead," Faust growled as he soothed Molly with long strokes to her back. "It's okay, Pixie. I'm not mad at you. I'm mad at the bastard who did this."

"Me, too," she whispered. And peeked up when neither man answered. Their shocked expressions made the corners of her mouth tilt up. She shook her head, unable to believe she could find anything humorous. "He scared me so bad."

"I'm going to get this cleaned up, Molly. We'll have to keep an eye on you. There's a lot of germs under someone's nails. It might be better to go to the ER for a shot of antibiotics," Doc suggested.

"I'm not going."

"Pixie. We need to listen to Doc. He knows his stuff," Faust suggested.

"No."

"Do what you can do," Faust said, looking at Doc. "Did someone call the police?"

"They just pulled up, Faust."

"Hold on, Doc. Let's let them see what that bastard did to her," Faust suggested.

Molly's head swam with exhaustion and an overload of emotions. She'd given her statement to the police. They'd asked to see her without Faust and she'd refused. When they'd had the gall to ask if someone in the Shadowridge Guardians had hurt her, she lost it.

"Are you kidding? I'm supposed to be safe at a church. Instead, some creep tries to pull me out of my car and leaves furrows in my skin. I came here because I knew Faust would protect me. Who falls for a lollipop-giving creep?"

"Lollipop?" one of the patrol officers asked.

"There's a report filed about this. I just got the results back from Officer Jimenez," Gabriel said, stepping forward with several sheets of paper.

The officer glanced at the lab report and then looked again. "Where did you get this lollipop?"

"It was the second one left under Molly's windshield wiper. She almost ate the first one, thinking it was from me. I found the second one," Faust said. "What's in it?"

The officer handed the report to Faust. The string of curses that erupted from his mouth made Molly hide her face in the curve of his neck. If it was that bad, she didn't want to know.

"Where were the lollipops left? At the church as well?" an officer asked, making notes.

"One at the church. One at her apartment," Faust growled, hugging her close. "Pixie, you never eat candy again without showing me."

Molly nodded.

"We don't know for sure that these two events are related," one officer warned.

When Faust snarled at him, Molly leaned back to pat his cheek. "The police officer didn't cause this. He's the good guy."

"We're going to visit the church and see what we can find out there. Perhaps, others in the area have seen something. Ma'am, I would suggest that you use extreme caution when going in and out of the church. Try to stay in a group," the officer suggested. "I've got the man's basic description from you. We'll increase patrols around the church and your apartment."

"She's staying here now," Faust told them.

"That's a good idea. Most people would think twice about causing trouble here," the cop agreed.

As the patrol men returned to their cars, Doc moved closer to clean her wounds. "Sure I can't get you to go to the ER?"

"No."

Doc looked at Faust for assistance.

"I'm not going to take her against her wishes. Not now. Is there anything you can do for her here?" Faust asked.

"I have some medicine here that will combat an infection. She's not going to like it," Doc told Faust, looking over Molly's head.

"Don't I get any word in this?" Molly asked, looking back and forth from her Daddy to Doc.

"Of course, Molly. What do you want to do? ER or Doc's office?" Faust asked.

"Doc's office," she stated unequivocally.

Faust lifted her from the workbench and cradled her in his arms, taking care not to brush her wounds. "Let's go."

Carrying her through the assembled crowd of Guardians and a few Littles who'd been attracted by the commotion, Molly put on a brave face and smiled at everyone. Who could be afraid of these guys? They looked tough and tatted, but each one of them would have put themselves in danger to help her.

"I won't tell," she whispered to Faust.

"What won't you tell, Pixie?"

"That you're all softies," she shared.

"Better not let that get out, Little girl. You'll ruin our reputations."

Molly saw the two men exchange looks and knew they'd decided she would be okay. As they walked through the clubhouse, Gabriel handed Faust a sippy cup. She took it eagerly from her Daddy and drank deeply, loving the cool water after all her tears.

"Thank you," she whispered over Faust's shoulder as he continued to move toward the hallway where their apartments were.

"I'm making spaghetti for dinner," Gabriel called back.

"Yum." Molly hummed against Faust's shoulder.

"You're in for a treat. Everyone loves Gabriel's spaghetti," Doc told her. He stopped just past Faust's apartment and opened a door on the opposite side. "Here's my office, Little girl. Faust, just set her on the table please."

Molly looked around. It looked just like an exam room. Faust set her on the exam table. There was that thing you looked into people's ears with on the wall along with a blood pressure cuff. She stared down at the metal footrests that were folded away. What kind of exams did Doc do?

Faust rubbed her back when she stiffened up straight. "You're okay, Pixie. Doc takes care of all the Guardians and their Little girls."

"Faust, we need to take her dress off to treat the wounds," Doc said softly.

"I'm afraid this dress may have seen better days, Pixie," Faust said as he swept her hair away to unzip the back of the dress.

"I can get the blood out. This is my best dress. I have to save it," Molly said urgently.

"We'll soak it in cold water when we get back to our room," Faust said, exchanging a glance with Doc.

"I know it doesn't look like much, but it's perfect to wear to work," Molly explained.

"I'm sure it's lovely without your blood scattered all over it," Doc said as the two men maneuvered her arm through the material, trying not to scrape her damaged skin against a seam or the zipper. The other arm was much easier to remove.

When Faust allowed the fabric to pool around her waist, Molly grabbed it with her good arm to hold it over her bra. "I don't need to take it off. You can see my arm this way, too."

"Doc has his reasons for wanting your dress off, Pixie." Faust lifted her bottom from the table by wrapping an arm around her waist. Doc quickly scooted the material over her legs and feet.

"I'm going to clean up your arm, disinfect it, and put some soothing ointment on it first, Molly. Does that sound okay?"

"Okay," she whispered, still not sure why she couldn't wear her dress. Molly did have to admit that the cool air felt good on her skin. She hadn't realized how overheated she felt.

"I have a job for you," Doc told her.

"What?" Her curiosity blossomed.

"I want you to take long breaths to relax and drink your water. You had quite a shock. Let's see if you can make your insides feel better while I work on the outside," Doc suggested.

Molly nodded. She rested back against Faust's supporting arm around her body and took a sip from her cup.

"That's perfect," Doc praised.

She felt like she should be more worried about being dressed only in her bra and panties but didn't. Deciding she wouldn't worry about that now, Molly basked in the feeling that she was safe, and they were taking care of her.

Doc bustled around gathering a basin and some gauze. He started cleaning off the blood that had run and smeared on her skin before turning to the gouges. "This may hurt. I'll be as gentle as I can, but I need to clean out these scrapes. Squeeze your Daddy's hand."

Faust held out a hand for her and she wrapped her fingers around his. Her hand looked like a doll's in comparison to his strong one. Molly started to giggle but winced as Doc started on the first scratch.

"Ouch!" she yelped.

"Can't you be more careful?" Faust demanded. His face hardened into a glower.

"This has to be done, unfortunately. Molly, distract your Daddy so he doesn't slug me. Squeeze his fingers hard if I treat a sore spot," Doc requested.

"He wouldn't do that," Molly protested before gasping when he hit a really sore spot.

The growl that came from her Daddy's throat made her squeeze his hand hard as she watched his expression.

"Whoa, Pixie. You almost disconnected my fingers," Faust protested.

"Doc told me to squeeze your fingers. Am I too strong?" Molly asked, playing innocent.

The snicker that came from the medic made her want to giggle, but Molly knew Faust hadn't recovered from her arrival.

"I'm sorry I scared you. I didn't know where else to go," Molly told him, squeezing his fingers as Doc worked. It helped— a bit.

"You did exactly the right thing. You can always get help here from the Shadowridge Guardians," Faust assured her.

"Even if we stop seeing each other?" Molly forced herself to ask. She couldn't see how this handsome man would want to stay with her.

"What are you talking about? First, you're my Little girl. If you decide I'm not the right Daddy and walk away, I won't have changed my mind. Second, the Guardians will protect you as long as I tell them to. Revoking your protection isn't going to happen," Faust declared.

"You might change your mind. I'm not very exciting to have in your life," Molly whispered.

"I'm not going to change my mind and I don't think my heart

can handle any more excitement than we've had this afternoon," Faust told her.

"But you might," Molly whispered.

"Have you met Faust?" Doc interjected. "Pigs are more likely to turn tie dye colored and drive limousines than Faust is to let you slip through his fingers. He's more stubborn than a mule."

"Doc," Faust warned.

"I'm just telling the truth." Doc defended himself easily and Molly guessed he knew Faust well and liked him despite all his rough edges. "All cleaned up, Molly. You did a very good job holding still. I'm going to smooth some ointment on it and wrap it up. This will feel much better. Keep drinking."

Obediently, Molly took another long drink as she watched Doc set the basin in the sink and change his gloves. When he returned to her side, he squeezed out a long dollop of ointment on a fresh piece of gauze. Gingerly, he dabbed on the cloudy concoction.

"That's nice." Molly sighed in contentment.

"There's some topical painkiller in here," Doc explained, holding out the tube. "Faust, I'm going to give this to you. No more than three times a day. If it's hurting badly, I need to see the wounds."

"Got it," Faust said without hesitation.

"Oh, I won't bother you," Molly rushed to add.

"You will if this hurts," Doc said sternly, making her gulp.

"Okay," she whispered.

He wrapped it in gauze and secured it with a piece of paper tape. "You were very good, Molly. That deserves a reward." He discarded his gloves and opened a drawer to pull out a wrapped item. "Your Daddy can open this for you."

Faust accepted it and said, "You never give me candy" as he opened it.

"You're never good," Doc zinged back.

"True," Faust admitted before holding out a candy ring that looked like a big red diamond. "This looks good."

Accepting it immediately, Molly popped it into her mouth and hummed in enjoyment. She didn't react when Doc pressed a hand against her forehead.

"You're too hot, Molly. I think we need to take your temperature. I'd hoped you'd cool off as I cleaned your arm."

"I am hot," she admitted, pushing her hair back with one hand.

"Faust, help Molly lay back on her side," Doc instructed.

"Hold this, too, Daddy," Molly said, extending the ring candy to him.

"You can suck on that, Pixie."

"Not if he's taking my temperature," Molly protested as Doc returned to stand behind her.

"Panties off," Doc announced before pulling her underwear down her body as Faust lifted her hips helpfully.

"What? No!" Molly whispered, appalled to be nude from the waist down in front of the two men. She drew her knees up to her stomach to hide.

"Perfect, Little girl. This will just take a few minutes," Doc announced as he pulled on new gloves before taking a thick tube out of a new package.

When he applied lubricant to the tip generously and put a dollop on his index finger, Molly realized what was going on. She tried to straighten her legs, but Faust held her securely in place.

"No silliness, Pixie. The doc needs to check your temperature."

"In my mouth, yes. In my bottom, never!" she hissed.

"Little girls should always have their temperatures taken in their bottoms," Doc explained. "You've been drinking cool water. That's not going to give me an accurate measurement. Close your eyes and enjoy your candy. Your Daddy is right here to keep an eye on me."

Molly turned her head to look at Faust who held her so firmly but gently. His face was lined with concern. He was worried about her. Slowly, Molly put the candy back in her mouth and closed her eyes.

"Thank you, Pixie," Faust told her softly.

She tried to concentrate on other things—the changes she needed to make on a certain file at work, what she was going to do about her apartment, and most of all, why had everyone's eyes widened in shock at the results of the lollipop analysis.

It was hard to think of anything else as Doc spread her bottom and pressed his finger against her small, hidden opening. She sucked furiously as he pressed the digit inside and rubbed it around the tight passage. The air gushed out of her lungs when he withdrew his touch. Her reprieve didn't last long.

"Just the thermometer," Doc explained as he pressed the thin cold instrument deep into her bottom.

He turned and twisted it to seat the tip. Each movement of the device inside her captured her attention. Molly squeezed her legs together, hoping the men couldn't see how aroused this was making her. Stop reacting to this treatment! Her body didn't listen.

"Faust, if this temperature is elevated, I'm going to give Molly some antibiotic suppositories. She'll need one morning and night for five days. Since she's moved in here, that should be fairly easy to accomplish."

"I've got it. Thanks, Doc."

After what felt like forever, Doc removed the thermometer and announced, "One hundred point five degrees, Molly. That's too high just for being upset. Your Daddy's going to give you medicine starting tomorrow morning. I'm going to give you a couple of things now: an antibiotic and a medicine to relax you and help you take a short nap to recover."

Doc moved around the room swapping out fresh gloves and pulling something from the locked cabinets. Molly peeked as he handed Faust a large container of huge pills. "I can't swallow those."

"These are suppositories, Molly. They go in your bottom.

Faust, you may want to put her in a pull-up for a few days to avoid accidents."

Before Molly could respond to all that, Doc spread her bottom once again and quickly pressed two large doses of medicine deep into her bottom. They were cool and thick inside her. Not as cold as the thermometer but she could definitely feel them. She tried to push them out.

"None of that, Molly," Doc reprimanded her. "I can see your muscles tensing. If you try to push the medicine out, I'll have to put a plug in your bottom."

"No!" she said, shaking her head.

"Will you be good and let your medicine work?" Doc asked.

"Yes," she whispered.

"Faust, she'll start feeling sleepy in a few minutes. Her body will absorb the medicine in her bottom quickly. Take her to your apartment and let her sleep for an hour. Wake her up for dinner and tuck her back in bed to sleep for the night," Doc told his MC brother.

"Take the candy out of her mouth," the medic warned and then laughed when Faust rolled his eyes so hard they almost made a sound. "Got it. You'll take good care of her."

In a short time, Doc handed Faust a bag of supplies to go along with the medicine container and her now empty sippy cup. The men wrapped Molly in a blanket which she immediately tried to push away.

"It's too hot," she said, rubbing her face with the hand that held her candy.

"I'll run fast across the hall and then we'll take it off, Pixie."

"Fast," she agreed, closing her eyes as she rested in Faust's arms.

Doc piled her clothing on her tummy and opened the door for Faust. Following them across the hall, he opened Faust's door as well. "Out of banana pudding, huh?"

"I knew you all would steal it."

"Damn, right," Doc agreed.

"I'll make everyone pudding," Molly promised.

"Another day, Pixie," Faust told her.

"Good idea, Daddy," she said, barely holding on to her stream of thoughts. "Tired. And my bottom is slick."

"There's nothing wrong with that, Little girl. Thanks, Doc," Faust said, walking inside his apartment.

"Anytime. Yell if you need me."

The door clicked behind him as Faust dropped the bag of supplies on the couch. He carried her to the bedroom and jostled her slightly in his arms as he pulled down the covers to lay her on the cool sheet. Unwrapping the blanket from around her, he quickly removed her bra, too.

Molly sighed with delight at the feel of the cool air on her heated body. She fought off the washcloth her Daddy wiped over her face. "No!"

"You're all sticky, Pixie. Hold still." He wiped her face and hand, removing her ring lollipop.

"I want that," Molly fussed.

"Let's try this." He held up the pacifier they'd chosen from the closet and popped it into her mouth.

"Mmmm." Molly hummed and turned on her side.

CHAPTER
FOURTEEN

Standing by her bed, Faust hesitated to wake Molly up. She'd fallen asleep so fast and hadn't moved for the last hour. Doc knew what he was doing. Faust sat on the edge of the bed and softly rubbed her back.

"Pixie? Can you wake up for Daddy?"

"Five more minutes," she mumbled, and the pacifier fell out of her mouth.

"Dinner's ready, Little girl," Faust told her as he picked it up before her questing hand could find it and pop it back in her mouth. "You don't want to miss Gabriel's spaghetti."

"Mmm, spaghetti," she mumbled.

"That's right. Do you like meatballs, Little girl?"

"Maybe if they're small. I don't like to gnaw on my food," she commented sleepily.

"I'll give you tiny bites," he promised.

"My arm is ouchie."

"Let's put some fresh ointment on it before we go do dinner."

Molly opened her eyes to peek at him. "Did they find that guy?" she asked.

"Not yet, Pixie. You'll stay here with Daddy, and I'll make sure you get to work and home safely."

"Does everyone think I'm silly?"

"For getting attacked and coming here for help? No way. They all think you're a superstar for getting away from that asshole," Faust assured her, trying to keep the anger from his voice and failing.

"I'm hungry," she admitted.

"Let's wash your face. Find something comfortable to put on. And make your arm feel better."

"And then eat spaghetti?"

"All you want."

Faust scooped her up in his arms and carried her to the bathroom. He set her on the toilet, and she automatically peed without thinking she should be embarrassed. He washed her face to keep her distracted.

After threading her feet into the pullups he'd gathered for her, Faust helped her stand before wiping the leftover lubricant from her bottom and throwing the washcloth in the hamper.

"Thank you," she said, turning lovely shades of pink.

Faust kissed her softly before pulling the lightly padded garment into place. "Your bottom may be a bit messy from the medicine. That's okay. It's expected. Daddy will take care of you. Okay?"

She nodded and leaned her head against his chest. "Maybe I don't need any more medicine. We could just tell Doc it's working."

"That's not going to happen. Let me wash my hands and we'll find something for you to wear."

"Can I wear one of your T-shirts?" she asked, hesitantly.

"Of course, Pixie. Want to wear a Shadowridge Guardian one?"

Her instant smile in response faded quickly. "Is that against the rules?"

"Not at all. You're my Little girl. You're part of the MC now," Faust assured her.

A few minutes later, Faust held her hand as they walked

slowly down the hallway. When the emerged into the large gathering area, Molly paused to see who was there. Faust bit his lip as he let out a string of curses in his mind. His desire to keep from scaring Molly—especially today—was the only thing that prevented them from escaping.

When she shrunk back, he knew his face was giving him away. Faust dropped down to one knee. "I'm sorry, Pixie. I'm not mad at you. I'm mad at the..." He paused as he tried to come up with a word that wasn't a curse word.

"Freaking a-hole?" she whispered a suggestion.

"Let's go with that. I'm pissed at the freaking a-hole who hurt and scared you. If I get my hands on him..." Faust balled up his free hand.

"We call the police and let them take care of it, Daddy." Molly patted his chest with her free hand.

He studied her earnest face and felt his blood pressure drop. "I'd rather pound him into the dirt," Faust admitted, knowing he'd never do that in front of Molly.

"Me, too. But that makes us the bad guys instead of him. I'm hungry, Daddy."

"Let's go get food in your tummy. Want me to carry you?"

"No. I can walk this time. I just needed to pull myself together."

He smiled at her sweet face. Leaning forward, Faust kissed her lightly before standing. He held out his hand for her once again and squeezed her fingers lightly when she slapped her hand down on his playfully. As they walked in, the other Littles slid off their Daddies' laps and met them halfway.

"Can we give you a hug?" Carlee asked.

"I'd love one," Molly admitted.

"Be careful of her arm," Faust warned, moving to her injured side to protect her.

One after another, the Littles in the room gave her gentle hugs and told Molly how glad they were that she was okay.

"Thanks, everyone," Molly said quietly.

"Come on. Gabriel made spaghetti. You're going to love it," Ivy shared.

"I'm starving," Molly admitted.

"Here's a seat," Gabriel called, pointing at an empty chair where several Daddies sat waiting for their Littles to return. "I just pulled some garlic sticks from the oven. How many can you eat?"

"Three," burst from Molly's lips, surprising everyone.

"I want to see that. Come on. I'll get you some," Gabriel said as he set a huge bowl of spaghetti on the table. "Here's your spaghetti."

Faust allowed Molly to pull him to that spot. Sitting down, he lifted her onto his lap and tucked a napkin into the neckline of their T-shirts. He plucked a bread stick from the basket Gabriel plopped in front of them and handed it to Molly. Immediately, she took a big bite and moaned as she chewed.

He'd heard that sound before. His body reacted instantly. Damn. I've got this bad.

"Try this, Daddy," Molly urged, pushing the stick to his lips. Obediently, Faust took a big bite, stealing almost all the rest of the bread in her hand and making her protest, "Daddy!"

"We'll get you more," Gabriel promised, sitting down at the table and lifting Eden onto his lap as he talked. "Eat the rest of that one and make your Daddysaurus get his own."

"Daddysaurus," she repeated and giggled.

"I will not be known as a Daddysaurus," Faust growled, shooting lasers from his eyes at the other people at his table as he twirled a few strands of spaghetti on his fork.

"Right," Kade drawled.

"Try this, Pixie," Faust said, holding the bite up to Molly's lips.

She opened her mouth and allowed him to feed her. A fraction of a second later, her eyes rolled back in her head as she chewed. "That's amazing!" she mumbled.

"No talking with your mouth full," Faust corrected her gently before wiping the sauce from the corner of her mouth.

Molly nodded eagerly and rubbed her tummy in the universal symbol of yumminess.

"Thank you, Molly. I'm glad you like it," Gabriel told her with a smile as he fed Eden.

Leaning back against Faust's powerful chest, Molly relaxed. Her arm ached but was okay. Doc's ointment made it better when it hurt. The bread sticks and spaghetti were like medicine, filling the emptiness inside. The warm conversation and friendliness of the group helped dull the scariness of her afternoon.

When they'd finished one bowl of spaghetti together and Faust had eaten another huge bowl himself, Molly wrapped her arms around Faust's thick bicep and hugged his arm to her chest. When he leaned down to check on her, she pressed a kiss to his cheek and whispered, "Thank you."

"For what, Pixie?" he asked quietly.

"Thank you for being my Daddy."

"I'm afraid I won't be letting you go," he told her seriously.

"I'm good with that."

"Time for you to go to bed, Harper," Doc said firmly.

"It's just eight," she protested.

"You almost couldn't get out of bed this morning. More sleep is just what you need," he said, laying down the law.

Harper opened her mouth as if she were going to complain and took one more look at her Daddy's face before nodding. "Night, everyone!"

"That's our clue, too, Little girl," Faust told Molly as he lifted her off his lap to stand next to him.

"I've got kitchen detail tonight," Fury called across the island. "Bring me any dishes left out there."

"I don't want to go, Daddy," Molly whispered. "I was having fun." She covered her mouth when a massive yawn surprised her.

"There will be more fun evenings," Faust promised. "Would you take this to Fury for me?"

She nodded and headed into the kitchen with their bowl as Faust followed with his arms full of breadstick baskets, glasses, and shakers of parmesan cheese. Fury took the dish from her hand and slid it into the sink filled with soapy water.

"Want to take some spaghetti for lunch tomorrow?" Gabriel asked as he dished up the leftovers.

"Yes, please."

"You've got it, Molly. I'll add a couple of breadsticks, too," the phenomenal cook promised.

"Thanks, Gabriel," Molly said with a smile as her Daddy led her back to his apartment.

"Their apartment." Molly corrected that mental thought.

"No! Get away!" Molly panicked, kicking and hitting to get away.

"Pixie. You're okay, Little girl. You're safe."

Opening her eyes, Molly stared into familiar brown eyes. It took a couple of seconds for her to process that she wasn't in danger and the hard body she was hitting as hard as she could was Faust. Tears poured down her face.

"I'm so sorry! Did I hurt you? I should go sleep in the other room. You should be safe in your own bed. Or... Maybe I should go back to my apartment."

"That's not happening."

"You don't deserve to be battered when you're trying to sleep," she said, totally appalled by her behavior, asleep or not.

"How well do you think I'd sleep if you weren't next to me?" he asked gently.

"Better than now," she guessed.

"Try again."

"You'd worry? You didn't seem like the worrier type when I met you," she pointed out.

The corners of his mouth twitched upward. "You didn't seem like a hugger, either," he teased.

"How can you be so nice?" she asked, searching his face.

"Don't tell anyone. It's our secret."

"I'm sorry, Faust. I've been nothing but trouble since you helped me."

"You are the best thing that has ever happened to me. Whoever this guy is out there who hurt you yesterday, his behavior is not your fault."

"Still now it's affecting you."

"I can take care of myself, Pixie. He's picking on you because he knows you're not going to turn around and put him on the ground. Not that you'd want to. He's not trying to give me candy."

She had to snort at that visual image. "Did I hurt you?"

"Badly. I could use a few kisses."

"You!" Molly couldn't help herself from grinning at him. "I think I owe you a billion kisses."

"You hit me right here," he said, pointing at a spot on his chest.

Quickly, she leaned forward and pressed her lips to his skin.

"And here." He tapped on his chin.

Molly didn't hesitate in soothing that owie as well. Wrapping her arms around his neck, she took the initiative to kiss his lips directly before whispering, "Make love to me, Daddy."

"Since we're both awake..." he said with a wolfish grin.

Wrapping his arms around her waist, he turned, lifting her body on top of his. He stroked his hands over her sides, guiding her up to sit straddling him. "You'll have to be up here where I can keep an eye on you at all times."

She could feel his body hardening against her, fueling her arousal as well. The view from above him was pretty darn fine as she traced his tattoos. The fiery look in his gaze was enough to reassure her that he found her body attractive and desirable. Molly pushed away her insecurities and moved her hips against him.

Crossing her fingers, Molly sent a tiny prayer up to heaven. "Thank you for sending me Faust," before enjoying the pleasures this amazing man lavished on her.

CHAPTER
FIFTEEN

Faust texted Molly on the hour. He'd wanted her promise to respond every half hour but had relented when she'd explained why that wouldn't be possible. With his phone set up facing him, he watched for his screen to light up with an incoming message as he forced himself to work.

"Faust, I've got a question for you about a motor." Kade strode in to stand braced against his counter.

"Move!" Faust roared.

Kade turned to see the phone behind him and smirked as he shifted out of the way. "I'm going to pretend you didn't just yell at your boss because I know you've got it bad, Daddysaurus."

Faust shook his head. "You're lucky I'm here." He deliberately didn't comment on his new nickname that had made it around the shop that morning.

"You wouldn't be here if that Little girl of yours hadn't promised to stay inside the church and only come out when you called this afternoon."

"You've got that right." Faust checked the screen again. No message. "Distract me. What did you need?"

"I've got someone at the front desk with a question about a rebuilt motor on a vintage bike. It sounds to me like a kit build, but he's assuring me it isn't. Could you see what you speak engine to him?" Kade asked.

"Let me send Molly a message and I'll follow you up."

"Perfect."

Little girl. You promised to answer me. If you want to sit down to type tomorrow...

Taking his phone, Faust headed for the front of the shop. There a man stood, looking around. He looked uncomfortable, like he wasn't used to being in a cycle repair shop.

"You had a question about a motor?"

"Yeah. You ever worked on something like this?" The man held up his phone, displaying a picture of something much different than a motorcycle.

With a roar, Faust rushed forward thrusting a forearm under the man's chin to drive him back against the supply shelves. He ignored the scattering of the customers from the waiting area. They didn't matter. Holding the threat pinned there by the neck, Faust felt the Guardians ring behind him without asking a single question. "Where is she?"

He eased up on the man's throat slightly to allow him to draw a breath and answer.

"You'll never find her without me," he rasped.

"That doesn't keep me from hurting you badly. Your tongue will still work if I start breaking bones." Faust moved quickly and ripped the phone out of the man's hand. He tossed it over his shoulder knowing one of his brothers behind him would catch it.

"Don't mess up his face. You know this piece of shit has his phone enabled for facial recognition," Kade said in a tone devoid of emotion that spoke volumes about how far he would go to back up Faust.

"I'm looking at the picture Faust. There's no indication that she's hurt. She looks surprised." Steele's voice came from behind him, cool, logical.

Faust's blood continued to boil. He wouldn't come down

from berserker mode until she was in his arms. "Grab my phone from my bench and call her."

"On it," Talon answered.

"He's starting to turn blue, Faust," Gabriel mentioned in a deceptively casual tone. Faust knew he must have seen the shop on the security camera.

"I don't fucking care," Faust snarled, not taking his eyes off the man in front of him.

"Me, neither," Gabriel admitted.

"It's ringing, Faust. I have it on speakerphone," Talon told him.

You've reached Molly's phone. Leave me a message and I'll call you back.

"Fuck!" Faust cursed. "You are dead if you've harmed a hair on her head."

The man swung an arm toward Faust's shoulder and the large man deflected it easily. The snap and muffled groan of the collateral damage for that move didn't quench the blood lust flowing through Faust's body. He was going to tear him apart bit by bit. That finger was nothing.

Blade was by his side in a flash. Armed with a thick zip tie, he restrained his arms behind his back as Faust held him pinned in place.

"That picture's in the office at her desk. Call the church. It's in my contacts," Faust ordered.

"Hello?" a shaky male voice answered.

"Where's Molly?" Faust demanded.

"I don't know. This is Minister Steve. A man just broke in here and tried to take her. I need to call the police."

"He doesn't have her?"

"I saw her running away. I tried to stop him. He knocked me down. I must have hit my head," the older man guessed. "Lester O'Brien was here. I don't see him now."

"Call the police. We're on our way," Steele advised. He

stepped away without hesitation. The men would take care of him. He had more important things to do.

"What do you want me to do with this dickwad?" Bear called from his seat on top the struggling visitor, after a short tussle.

"Tie him to something. Will you stay with him, Bear, Gabriel?" Steele threw over his shoulder as they ran for their bikes.

"We're missing the fun," Gabriel told Bear as he finished tethering his feet to one of the motorcycle lifts.

"Ummm. Is everything okay? Should we leave?" one of the customers who'd been in the waiting room asked.

"You're fine. They're just taking a break," Bear assured them as he rose smoothly to his feet and headed for a phone. "There will be a bit of a delay in finishing your tune-up."

"Good af…" the rest of that word disappeared from her brain as Molly looked up to see the visitor to the church office. Reaching out automatically for her keys, Molly bolted to her feet and heard her office chair clatter noisily to the tiled floor.

"Molly? Are you okay?" Minister Steve called from his office.

"Call the police," she yelled as she backed away, recalling the familiar man in front of the waist high counter that separated them.

"More of those hoodlums visiting?" Lester suggested as he walked back from the kitchen at the rear of the office space with a coffee pot full of water. He was still fuming that Molly wasn't making and bringing him coffee.

"That is the man who assaulted me yesterday and has left drugged candy on my car," Molly answered, angling her path to disappear into the private area.

"What? This guy doesn't look like he'd hurt a fly." Lester scoffed, continuing to the coffee pot. He fit the water-filled tank back into place before picking up a fresh coffee mug.

"Yeah, Molly. I couldn't hurt a fly," the man repeated as he opened the swinging gate that allowed access to the space behind the counter.

"Stop right there, young man. This is a church. We will not tolerate any violence or shenanigans here," Minister Steve told him, gripping the gate to prevent him from walking through.

"Right," the man drawled sarcastically before backhanding the minister to knock him out of the way.

Molly saw him tumble and strike his head. That sickening thump of his head against the wall forced her to move. She darted past Lester and ran down the hallway. Hearing the crash of a ceramic coffee cup behind her, she suspected that Lester had dropped his coffee, shocked by the intruder's treatment of their boss.

Turning her head to see how close the man was to her, Molly spotted Lester running behind her. She skidded to a stop at the back door. It led back into the storage areas of the church and was kept locked. She fumbled with the keys in her pocket and looked down to find the right one for that deadbolt.

Glancing over her shoulder to see where the man was, Molly could see him stalking down the hallway as if he had all the time in the world. The look on his face was of a hunter triumphantly cornering his prey. She forced herself not to panic and scanned the keys.

"Molly, you've led me on a merry chase…" he called.

"Stop right there. This space is only for church officials and employees," Lester warned, holding his arms out to the sides to block as much of the hallway as possible.

The key almost sparkled as she spotted it. Pushing it quickly into the lock, she rotated it until she heard the click. She twisted the doorknob and dragged it open. Her heart wouldn't let her abandon the assistant minister. "Quick, Lester. Come on."

"Go call the authorities, Molly."

Go back to the office to get to the phone?

The sight of the man launching into a run made her dart through the doorway and keep running. Molly's heart pounded in her throat as she forced herself through the dark storage area. With any luck, he wouldn't find the lights. The switches were partially concealed by the extra shelves that had been put up over the years.

Taking off her shoes, Molly walked as quickly and silently as possible. After turning a corner, Molly paused for a few precious seconds to pull a set of cushions from a stack under the shelves to scatter on the ground. If he fell, she'd have more time.

If she could get to the door that led to the baptismal pool, Molly could crawl through the curtained area to get to the sanctuary and out the door. She cursed that there was no phone along her path. Maybe Faust would figure out something was wrong.

"Oh, Molly. They say smoking is bad for your health," the man called, and she looked over her shoulder to see the flickering glow of a small flame.

Of course, he has a lighter!

He was too close. There was no way she could get try the keys on her keyring and find the right one quickly enough. She wouldn't make it into the baptism area. Trying to remember where everything was, Molly sunk to the floor and felt along the items on the bottom row.

Please, let there be a space big enough for me to fit into.

Praying with all her heart, she pushed one large item and it shifted. Thank you! The small Christmas tree! They'd almost forgotten to put it up in the children's area a few years ago because it got pushed back out of sight. Molly had always placed it carefully at the edge of the deep shelves so it wouldn't get overlooked.

She grabbed the gold candlestick on the shelf above the box. Feeling the intricate decorations biting into her palm, she forced herself to move. Unable to stop herself from looking as she backed into the disguised space, Molly could see the light getting brighter. He was almost to her. Holding her breath, she closed her eyes and prayed.

CHAPTER
SIXTEEN

F aust spotted a police car coming from the opposite direction as turned his bike into the church parking lot.
He pulled his bike close to the door and kicked the stand down with the other Shadowridge Guardians at his back.

"Stop right there," the officer called from his patrol car.

Faust ignored him and ran for the door. Ink, King, Kade, and Bear followed him into the building. Faust heard Steele's voice explaining.

"Officer, there was a break in. They're after…" Steele's voice cut off as the door slammed closed.

Faust ran to the office. The older minister pointed down the hallway and Faust didn't wait for an explanation. He jumped over a man slumped by the wall and continued through the open door. The passage was dark.

"Molly, I'm here!" he shouted into the gloom. He didn't care if the man knew he was there. Nothing was going to get between him and Molly.

A chuckle came from the obscurity before him, sending a chill down his spine. It was muted. Distant? He moved quickly to close the distance.

"What's your endgame, dickwad? The police are in the

parking lot. Unfortunately for you, so are my brothers," Faust called as he stalked forward.

"The police won't let them put a hand on me."

"I hope there's an exit in front of you, you piece of shit. Otherwise, you have to come back through me," Faust pointed out.

"Molly's going to be my ticket out of here."

Going to be. He doesn't have her. He took several steps forward toward the corner that separated them to get a better idea where the other man was. Turning the corner, he peered into the darkness, straining his ears for a whisper of a sound.

"If I don't get her now, I'll get her the next time I get out," a voice answered, still at a distance.

How fucking big is this storage area?

"Out of what?" Faust asked, trying to keep him talking so he could locate him. Turning another corner, he saw a faint glow flickering. A flame. The bastard can see.

"Jail. The bitch reported me for disciplining my wife and kids. I'm young. I've got plenty of years to get revenge. I can play the game to get parole—again."

He felt Kade's hand close over his shoulder in a silent warning. Faust forced himself not to lose control. Get Molly safe. "A man's house is his kingdom. Women need to understand that."

"Exactly. So, I'll teach Molly a lesson and she'll understand." The man's voice was close.

He turned to hiss into Kade's ear. "Find the fucking light switch. Light this up!"

"I'm afraid I have a problem with that," Faust commented. "You involved me and the Shadowridge Guardians with your messenger."

"My brother does anything I want. He's family. He just brought a picture to warn you. They won't be able to pin anything on him. Then, when I go back to trial, he'll locate my wife and kids when they have to testify against me. She fled without leaving a forwarding address for some reason."

"You wanted to get caught?"

"Sure. I have one thing left to do now before they lock me up. Come out, come out, wherever you are, Molly."

The sound of her name coming out of that jerk's mouth was the last straw. Faust burst around the corner and raced the last few feet to tackle the man who'd dared hurt his Little girl. Pain lanced through his side as he tackled him to the ground. Pushing that inconvenience from his mind, Faust captured the man's hand holding the knife and pushed it to the ground as King, Bear, and Kade rounded the corner, filling the wide hallway with muscular, pissed-off bikers.

White lights blazed from the ceiling and thundering steps raced down the passage toward them. Ink turned the last corner and skidded to a stop as he took in the trio restraining one man. "I miss all the fun."

"Youngest member had to flip on the lights," Kade explained, making Ink shake his head.

"Come out," the police yelled.

"We've got him," Ink bellowed to answer. "Faust? Did you know you're bleeding?"

A box slid out from the bottom shelf and two small hands appeared. One gripped a gold rod so tightly her knuckles were white. Molly's head and body followed as she scrambled from the hiding spot. She clambered to her feet and circled way around the man who'd chased her to reach Faust as he pushed himself against the wall to power himself to his feet.

"Daddy!" She ran toward Faust and tried to help him stand.

"Stay where you are, Faust. You've been stabbed. Do you want to bleed out?" King demanded.

The edges of Faust's vision darkened. He eased himself back down to the concrete floor. If he fainted, he'd never hear the end of it.

Molly hovered over him, trying to help, still holding the cylindrical object in her hand. Faust could see her shaking. "He put a knife in you?" she whispered.

"I'm fine, Pixie. Don't worry. A few stitches and..."

Faust stopped trying to reassure her as she stood up straight and turned to face the man held against the floor. A patrolman reached them with his gun in his hand as she took steps forward and raised the object in her hand.

"Freeze," the officer ordered, pointing the gun at Molly.

"He hurt them," she whimpered. "Over and over. I could hear his wife begging him to stop and her screams when he turned his attention to her instead. He's evil. Now he has this whole plan to take me out and find his ex-wife and kids to beat again? He should not take another breath in this world."

The police officer moved to get a clear shot as Molly moved closer to the man, raising the object in her hand higher. Faust heaved himself to his feet and wrapped his arms around his Little girl. "Someone else will judge him, Pixie. This isn't up to you."

"He's never going to stop coming after me," she whispered.

"He will. Ivy will make sure of it," Faust assured her, holding out his hand. Seeing the black fog growing denser, he locked his knees. King stood up from his position holding the man securely and shifted behind Faust.

"Ivy." Molly sighed her name and smiled. She placed the object in Faust's hand.

Faust heard the clatter as the rod slid through his limp fingers to hit the floor and felt King's arms wrap around his chest, pulling him back to settle on the floor.

"Daddy." Molly's sweet voice made him smile.

"I need an ambulance. Can someone clue me in? What is going on?" The policeman's voice sounded totally baffled.

Faust shifted and immediately heard the squeak of a chair. He felt her cold hands next as she rubbed his forearm.

"I'm okay, Pixie."

"You scared me," she admitted, holding his hand.

"I just wanted another scar to make you think I was tough." Faust tried to make light of his injury.

"I already know you're tough."

"I'm keeping weapons out of your hands," he tried to joke.

"He deserves a taste of his own medicine."

"Not at your hands. You'd never forgive yourself if you hurt someone," Faust gently pointed out.

"You're right."

"Climb into bed with me, Little girl. I need to hold you," Faust urged.

"I don't want to hurt you. Besides, there's an alarm on your bed. I just sat on it and the nurse came in to yell at me."

Faust felt his eyebrows draw together in concern. "She shouted at you."

"It's okay, Daddy. She was afraid I'd hurt you. Look, I pulled my chair way up. I can sit here and talk to you." Molly demonstrated by plopping down on the thinly cushioned chair.

"Totally not acceptable. How long are they keeping me in this hellhole?" Faust growled.

"I thought I heard your dulcet tones. I'm Margerie, your nurse. It's time for pain meds. Rate your pain for me on a scale of one to ten."

"Zero."

"You're lying," Margerie commented bluntly.

"Just tell her the truth."

"Three," he said and winced as he tried to shift in bed.

"A three from the bad biker dude. That must be a six on the regular people scale," the nurse commented as she injected medicine into his IV.

"Probably," Molly agreed with her.

Glaring at them both, Faust asked, "When do I get out of here?"

"A couple of days probably. There's a lot of stuff that can go wrong after you're stabbed. The doctor will tell you more, but you must have been very lucky that knife didn't cause more damage. You shouldn't be awake to glower at me."

Molly sniffed, and Faust looked over to see tears streaming down her face. "I'm okay, Pixie."

"I was so scared."

"There's an alarm on this bed?" Faust growled, looking at the nurse.

"There is."

"Take it off," he demanded.

"That's against protocol," she said crisply as she checked all the bags hanging from his IV pole.

"Somehow, I'm holding Molly. Here where I don't move or over there," he said, pointing to a chair.

"Fine." The nurse turned to look at Molly, who had tears streaming down her face by this time. "Don't hurt him."

"Yes, ma'am." Molly nodded eagerly.

"I didn't do this. You figured it out yourself," the nurse said, pushing a button on the side of the hospital bed before leaving the room.

Faust saw the corners of her lips curve up as she turned away. He switched his attention to Molly. "Come here, Pixie. I need to hold you."

Bolting to her feet, she almost knocked over the chair. Molly rounded the bed and hesitated before crawling carefully over the sheets toward him.

Faust wrapped his arm around her and held her against his body. He took a corner of the sheet and wiped her face dry. "No more tears. I'm fine. Is that asshole in jail?"

"He is. The police will be here some time to talk to you."

"I'll be glad to talk to them as well," Faust said ominously.

"It's not their fault the jerk is working the system. Hopefully, he won't get out again for a long time. Minister Steve and Lester are pressing charges. Ivy's getting everything tied up in a neat bow," Molly said.

A thought popped into his mind, and he asked, "The Guardians didn't leave you at the hospital alone, did they?"

"Oh, no. There has always been someone with me. I just sent everyone back to the compound so you could sleep," Molly explained. "Kade told me to tell you not to worry about work. Ink's filling in on engines."

The string of curses that flew out of his mouth made his Little giggle. Faust looked at her and said, "That's a joke?"

"Kade said that would make you get better faster. He didn't warn me your foul language would sizzle my eyebrows off," Molly teased.

"Sorry, Pixie."

"I hear voices. That's a great sign."

Molly tried to shift away at the sound of Minister Steve's voice, but Faust held her in place. "Stay."

"Thank you for stopping by. I'll be back at work soon," Molly promised when Steve came into the room.

"The office will survive without you for a few days, Molly. I think you're right where you need to be," Steve commented.

"How are you and Lester?"

"We're fine. Lester has a big goose egg on his forehead. He's enjoying all the attention."

"I didn't know how he got hurt until the Shadowridge Guardians filled in everything that happened as I tried to hide," Molly told him. "You tried to stop him, too. I'm sorry I brought trouble into the church."

"A house of God should be a refuge for everyone. The blame rests fully on the person that chooses to do evil. I stopped by today to check on you, young man."

Faust barely controlled a snort from shooting from his nose. Young man? "I'm doing fine."

"Are you religious?" the minister asked him directly.

"I believe in a higher power," Faust answered vaguely.

"Just not in a church. I understand, Faust. I'll invite you to attend a service with Molly. See if we can change your mind. In the meantime, I'd like to say a prayer for you to heal quickly. Totally selfish, of course. I need my secretary back at her desk."

Faust looked at Molly and knew this was important to her. "Thank you, Steve. I'll take any help I can get."

CHAPTER
SEVENTEEN

"Is he always this stubborn?" the nurse asked Molly.

"I'm not getting into that wheelchair," Faust stated flatly.

"It's hospital policy, sir. You'll be free of all our regulations just outside the front doors."

"I'm not getting into that wheelchair," Faust repeated for the fifth time.

"Ummm, Faust? Will you play a game with me?" Molly asked.

"If it involves me in that wheelchair, no."

"Even if we do a swap? You know, you get in the wheelchair so this wonderful nurse can go take care of sick people, and I'll owe you a favor," Molly suggested.

"What kind of a favor?" he asked, laser focused on her.

"I'm going to leave that up to you."

He studied her face for a couple seconds. When she winked, he swore "Fuck me" and sat down. "Give me that."

After handing him the huge, colorful floral arrangement the Littles had all made Atlas order for them, Molly trailed after them as the nurse walked briskly down the hall to the elevator. The Guardian in charge of the accounts had paid the bill without comment as he tried not to laugh, picturing Faust's reaction when that was delivered. Molly had prevented him from ordering a teddy bear addition to the flowers but had allowed the chocolate-covered strawberries. They had been delicious.

She was thankful for the hospital's skill in patching Faust up. They needed a break from the irascible biker who'd been ready to go home after surgery. The nurse patted her arm in a silent thanks as they stood in the elevator.

As the automatic doors opened, Molly slapped a hand over her mouth. Steele, Kade, and Storm sat on their bikes with their Littles hugging them tight. Right behind the line of cycles, Atlas stood by the open passenger door of Steele's black truck.

"Someone stab me again," Faust hissed.

"None of that. Look, your friends are here," the nurse said, locking the wheelchair's brakes.

Faust rose as quickly as his wound would allow and walked to the truck. Atlas plucked the flowers from his hands. "I'll take that, brother. These are beautiful. I bet they made your icky hospital room colorful."

"You helped them with that, huh?" Faust said with a glare.

"I was glad to fund your cheeriness," Atlas said. "Need help climbing up?"

"For fuck's sake," Faust said, stepping back to help Molly into the truck's back seat before swinging himself up into the passenger seat.

"Thank you, Atlas, for picking us up," Molly said cheerfully as he climbed into the truck.

"You're welcome, Molly."

The cycles took off in a roar of high-powered motors. Atlas followed them out of the drive and onto the street leading to the compound. As they passed parking lots, a Guardian or two joined the procession.

Molly watched Faust look in the side mirror as more joined the group. Thrilled by the thundering assembly, Molly's eyes filled with tears. These guys were brothers. They supported each other during the good times and the bad times. How had she ever thought they were scary?

"We're a fucking parade," Faust said, shaking his head.

"I want to learn to ride a bike," Molly said, patting her Daddy's shoulder. "Maybe just short trips for a while."

"The doctor told you I shouldn't ride my cycle for an extended time," Faust guessed.

"Oh, no. I'm sure you have to get used to riding on a motor-cycle," Molly said quickly.

"Lying will get your bottom spanked," Faust reminded her.

"So true," Atlas teased.

"Okay, so he said use care when riding," Molly admitted.

"I'll teach you, Pixie. We'll start this afternoon."

"Maybe tomorrow?" she suggested.

"There's not a fucking party at the clubhouse, is there?" Faust said, glaring at Atlas.

"No party," Atlas assured him.

"Someone has their head out of their ass."

"Bear's making you ribs, Daddy."

"Damn, that sounds good. If I never have hospital food again, it will be too soon," Faust grumped.

In a few minutes, they walked into the clubhouse. Streamers trailed from the rafters and a big welcome home sign hung over the kitchen. The smells coming from the covered dishes made Molly's mouth water.

"No party?" Faust said, pinning Molly with a steely look.

"It's a barbeque, Daddy. That's totally different than a party."

"You're lucky I'm hungry."

"Yay!" Molly said, dancing around him as Atlas plucked the vase from his hands to place on the end of the bar.

Faust loaded his plate with ribs and all the fixins' a few minutes later. He met the gaze of Bear who refilled the serving dishes as they emptied out. "We'll talk about this party later."

"Barbeque," Bear corrected him with a laser look. "Besides, we didn't do it for you." He looked over at Molly who had joined all the other Littles as they learned a new line dance from Talon. He'd insist she get a plate soon, but for now, she needed some fun after days of being in the hospital.

"Thank you for taking care of her," Faust said, instantly understanding the message.

"The Shadowridge Guardians take care of our own," Bear said easily.

"We do," Faust answered and headed for the chair he'd claimed for his own. He grabbed a beer on the way over. Popping the top, he swallowed gratefully. He'd refused pain killers after that first day, not liking how foggy they made his brain.

He looked at Steele. "What's Ivy say about that jerk?"

"She's working on a legal loophole to keep him in jail for the max sentence this time without the chance of parole. His ex-wife and kids are safe and won't be returning to town. She'll have a few more years to know he's locked up and her kids can grow up safely."

"And the brother who showed up here?" Faust asked. He wasn't going to forget that asshole's role.

"In the county jail for aiding and abetting," Steele assured him.

"Can I get some help moving Molly out of her apartment next week?" Faust forced himself to ask. He didn't want to rip the stitches out of the healing wound and delay his full recovery.

"You got it. We need you in the shop," Kade stated.

"I'll be there tomorrow."

"Good," Kade answered.

"Get help when you move the engines," Kade ordered. When Faust scoffed, Kade added, "Or I'll give you a permanent assistant. I'm sure there's a prospect who's never worked on an engine before that would jump at a chance to learn everything you know."

"Fuck off. You're not going to do that," Faust said, feeling the corners of his lips turn up. "I'll get help for a while."

"You're smiling, Daddy. Home is a good place, isn't it?" Molly asked and plucked a rib from his plate before scrambling up on Faust's lap on the good side.

"Hungry now?" he asked.

"How about we finish your plate and then you can get more?" she suggested.

"And a big gooey brownie for you?" Faust suggested.

"Gabriel made brownies? I'll just start with dessert," Molly said, wiggling forward.

"Food first. Then dessert, Little girl," Faust decreed, holding her in place. While she pouted, he scooped up a bite of potato salad. "Try this."

"Ooo! That's better than Miss Marcie's potato salad she brings to church socials."

"You should eat more. I wonder if the coleslaw is good?" Faust asked.

"I'll try it," Molly offered eagerly, relaxing back against him.

As he fed her, Faust looked around at everyone gathered and wondered who would find their Little next.

"There's a big birthday party coming up, Daddy. We have to go shopping for the best present for _____," Molly told him. "What do you think she'd like? I was thinking about getting her some clothes for _____."

"I think that would be a good idea. I bet we could order some online," Faust suggested, crossing his fingers.

"Oh, no, Daddy. We have to go to the store to feel the material and make sure it's soft. Stuffies don't like scratchy things," Molly told him.

"Of course not. We'll go. That would be a good trip on the

motorcycle," he suggested, thinking it wasn't too far to the mall and not horrible traffic.

"Are your trunk things big enough?" Molly asked.

"Saddlebags, Pixie. How many sets of clothes are you going to get?"

"Just one. But there are shoes and hats and…"

"We'll have plenty of room. We can even get you a leather jacket to ride on the bike."

"Can I have a patch?" she asked eagerly.

"We'll talk about it."

"Yay!" she cheered.

"Try some chicken, Pixie," Faust suggested, handing her a chicken wing.

"Yum. Daddy, I had a dream last night. Storm was in it."

"I don't think I like you dreaming about other men, Little girl."

"No, it wasn't that kind of dream. Storm was there and he was watching someone."

"Someone bad?" Faust probed.

"I don't think so. He looked… interested."

"That was an intriguing dream."

"Not as good as the dream I had about you later," Molly whispered, feeling her cheeks heat with embarrassment at even mentioning it.

"And I now know what I want to use my favor on," Faust declared.

"Daddy!"

A few minutes later, she admitted in an oh-so-quiet whisper, "I made banana pudding just in case you wanted to reenact my dream. It's only on day one, but it will be good."

When he stared at her hard, obviously connecting the dots between her spicy dream and banana pudding, Molly tried to look innocent as she wiped a finger down his chest before leaning in to lick that sensitive spot at the base of his neck.

Faust boosted Molly to her feet and set his plate in the chair after rising. "Life is short. We should have dessert first."

EPILOGUE

Molly held Faust's hand as they walked into the church. She could feel how tense he was. She squeezed his fingers as a couple came up to greet her.

"Molly! I'm so glad to hear you're okay. Minister Steve gave us a quick wrap up of what happened. You're so brave to have stood up for that woman and her children," the older woman told her.

"Oh, I just called the police." Molly tried to deflect the attention away from her.

"That's not how we heard it. Who's this strapping man with you?" her husband asked, looking up at Faust.

"This is Faust. He's my… boyfriend," Molly explained.

"Uh, huh. That pause means she likes you a lot more than that," the man said, smiling up at Faust. "You treat her well. We all love Molly."

"I will."

"Let me ask you a question. I've been thinking about getting a tattoo. What do you think of…"

Molly struggled to control the laughter that gathered inside her at the shocked look on Faust's face. Another couple joined them. And the man asked Faust a question about motorcycles. The congregation was all trying to make him feel welcome. Her heart grew about three sizes bigger with love for all of them.

"He's cute. He looks stern, but I bet he's a softie inside," one of their wives said to Molly with a nudge.

"I heard he threw himself in harm's way to make sure you were safe when that man broke in."

"He likes me," Molly admitted. "I think I'll keep him."

"How did you get him to church?"

"Minister Steve invited him," Molly shared.

Ahs and knowing nods followed. Minister Steve was known for getting people to do the right thing. He had a talent for saying just the right thing.

A chime signaled everyone they needed to take their seats. Molly and Faust settled next to the aisle in the back where the crowd was sparser. She felt him relax a bit. Sliding her hand back into his, Molly squeezed his hand before pulling the hymnal from the rack in front of them. She grinned up at him when he helped her turn it to the correct page.

She looked up at him when he joined in the singing and loved his deep voice. He was going to have to sing with her during the next karaoke night at the compound. He shook his head as if he could read her thoughts.

The sermon was light and uplifting. Minister Steve dealt with tough topics when he needed to but preferred to inspire instead of preaching brimstone and fire. Molly leaned back against the pew and enjoyed the fellowship that swirled around them.

A strangled sound came from the front. Lester stood from his chair near the pulpit and grabbed his chest. As he fell, everyone gasped and rose to their feet.

"Someone call 911. Is there a doctor here?" Minister Steve requested as he moved to kneel next to his assistant minister.

No one moved. Faust stepped into the aisle and called back

to Molly. "Call for an ambulance." He ran to the man who'd collapsed and started CPR.

"Thank you, Faust," Minister Steve said after the emergency vehicles left.

"Thank goodness you brought your friend," a churchgoer said before shaking Faust's hand. "Come back next Sunday. We like to have new blood in the church. It keeps us alive."

Molly knew Faust needed to escape all that attention. "I think I'd like to go home now, Faust."

He nodded and steered her out of the crowd.

When they got to her car, Molly stayed quiet as he wedged himself into her compact and drove from the parking lot. "Thank you for saving him. I heard the paramedics tell you he wouldn't have survived until they got there if you hadn't kept his heart beating."

"Don't tell the Guardians," he growled.

"You might be in the paper tomorrow," she suggested. "That last man that shook your hand owns The Daily Star."

"Fuck!" Faust cursed.

Molly stayed quiet for a few seconds before snickering. "They took a picture, too, while you were working on him. An action shot…" Laughter burst from her lips as he turned to stare at her with a look of horror on his face.

"We may have to change your name to something more in tune with your current hero status. What do you think of Saint?" she asked.

"I am going to spank your cute bottom," Faust swore.

"I'll look forward to it," she quipped.

As they parked in the Shadowridge Guardians' compound, Molly turned to Faust and shared, "I love you, Daddy."

The look on Faust's face made her heart skip a few beats. He reached for her and cursed the small space. "You had to tell me you love me inside a tin can."

She cracked open her door and waved at the space outside the car. Molly didn't dare get out herself. She'd learned that lesson. Faust shook his head and climbed out. In a few seconds, he'd circled the car and tugged Molly out.

"Say it again."

"I love you, Daddy."

He lifted her up to press a soft kiss to her lips. The second followed quickly as Molly wrapped her arms and legs around him to hold on. The sweet tender exchange made tears gather in her eyes.

"I love you, too, Molly."

"I know. You show me every day," she whispered and kissed him again. "I was so proud of you today. Not just for helping Lester, but for going to church with me. It was way out of your comfort zone. You were so brave."

"It wasn't like I was going to get stabbed again there. I don't think that older lady with the fancy blue hair was going to shiv me when I walked in the door for being on her turf," he scoffed.

"No stabbing," Molly agreed. "That's pretty well a no no in the bible. It won't be that exciting next time. If you want to go back."

"I'm with you, Pixie. Where you go, I go."

"Could we go back to your apartment?" she asked, giving him an over-the-top theatrical wink.

He gave her a hard kiss as he started walking. Everyone looked up when he threw the door open with one hand to carry Molly inside. Silence greeted them at their rushed entrance. Busy kissing her Daddy, Molly waved before they disappeared down the hallway. She had to smile against his lips as the sound of clapping followed them down from the main room.

"I'm going to church next week if it's that inspiring," Steele commented drily.

"Fuck," Faust said as he juggled her to open the door. "I'm never going to hear the end of this. And this is our apartment now. We're emptying out your place next week."

"Whatever you say, Daddysaurus."

Printed in Great Britain
by Amazon